# ASUNDER

## Iron Bulls MC #1

### PHOENYX SLAUGHTER

# COPYRIGHT

Asunder (Iron Bulls MC #1)
by Phoenyx Slaughter
Digital ISBN13 # 978-0-9907945-8-5
Paperback ISBN# 978-1-943950-75-1
Copyright © 2015 by Phoenyx Slaughter
All rights reserved.
Originally published May 3, 2015

Published by: Ahead of the Pack, LLC
Edited by: Hot Tree Editing and PREMA
Cover Designed by: AJ Lake

Asunder

IRON BULLS MC #1

**Karina**

For most of my life, I thought Logan and I were meant to be together. I loved him with everything I had.

He broke my heart.

Then I met Dante, and the perfect plan to get even with Logan began to form in my mind.

Dante is older, dark, dangerous, and the Sergeant-at-Arms of the Iron Bulls MC.

The same MC Logan joined when he left me.

This is going to be fun.

**Dante**

Karina Rivers was supposed to be a one-time afternoon distraction. I'm way too old and twisted for someone as innocent as her.

I want her anyway.

She doesn't realize she has the power to tear my MC apart.

# CHAPTER ONE

### Karina

ALTHOUGH THE FELT OF THE POOL TABLE IS starting to chafe against my bare back, the face planted between my legs has a magical tongue attached to it, so I'm not about to complain.

Firm fingers dig into my thighs, pulling me closer. This man is insatiable. Devouring me, not giving a shit about the wet, slurpy sounds echoing through the cavernous room of his clubhouse.

Not that it matters. For the moment, we're alone.

This is my first time inside the Iron Bulls MC's clubhouse.

"Whatcha got here, Dante?"

Dante, that's magic tongue's name. I whine and bump my hips up when he stops licking me to answer whoever interrupted him.

"None of your business. Get lost."

"You got her laid out in the front room. That's beggin' to have someone join in."

Even though it isn't phrased as a question, I think he's asking permission. Dante flicks his simmering brown eyes up at me then slips a finger inside my pussy. "She's a tight little bitch." My eyes roll shut and I let out a moan.

"Jesus, fuck! Karina? What the hell?"

My eyes snap open.

*Logan.*

"You know her, Hemi?"

"Yeah, I fuckin' know her."

Logan comes into my line of sight and my skin heats up with shame. My breasts are partially out, my skirt up around my waist, thighs spread wide, and Dante's fingers are still stroking me.

This is embarrassing.

But not surprising.

I'd known exactly what I was doing when I hopped on the back of Dante's bike this afternoon after school. I "accidentally" bumped into the big, frightening biker outside the liquor store. I couldn't have planned it better.

Except, I'm not getting the satisfaction I expected from the experience.

"Take her mouth. I'm busy down here." Then Dante disappears between my thighs again. I can't help moaning and arching my back up.

Logan stands over me. "Fuck, you even legal, yet?" he mutters.

"Never stopped you before," I whisper.

"Jesus." He rubs his hand over his face, and glances at Dante. He doesn't seem to be able to make up his mind.

2

Finally, he unbuckles his belt and pulls his cock out. He strokes himself from root to tip, then traces his fat cockhead over my lips. "Open."

Below, Dante takes my clit, sucking it into his mouth and I gasp. Logan uses the opportunity to shove his cock in my mouth.

I reach over and grab him, sucking him down harder.

"Fuck, girl."

Dante stands, tugging me down the table, before plunging into me with his thick cock. I scream around Logan.

"Watch your teeth, Karina," he warns.

Dante has a firm grip on my hips as he pumps into me with ruthless strokes. "You gonna come for us, lil' girl?"

I whine and nod my head.

"Get him off first. Let me see what a good little cumguzzler you are."

I can do that. I remember very well what Logan likes. I focus my attention on him, even as pleasure blooms through my body. His taste is familiar and brings a rush of memories—some sweet, some horrible. In no time, he's giving up his thick, salty cum and I swallow it down in great, greedy gulps. He rubs his thumb over my cheek as he pulls out, tucking his cock away. The look on his face is unreadable.

"Hot, fucking, lil' bitch, ain't you?" Dante grunts as he pounds into me. One hand slips from my hip, so his thumb can rub my clit. With Logan taken care of, I'm free to close my eyes and let Dante overwhelm my senses. He continues rubbing my clit in precise circles, while slamming into me.

"Good. Fucking. Girl. Tight as hell." His fingers are

3

digging into my hips, but I like the way he makes me feel. I gasp and twitch as he keeps working me over. "That's right, come for me. Come on my cock, you hot little bitch."

I'm floating as I shatter and fall back down to Earth.

LATER WE'RE in Dante's bedroom. In his bed. My dress hit the floor the minute we stepped inside.

"Decided I don't want to share you with anyone else while you're here, babe."

I like the sound of that. How many times had I wished Logan felt that way?

"You need to be anywhere?" he asks.

"No. My dad's out of town, so I'm good as long as I get to school on time."

He draws back with a quizzical expression. "School?"

Heat floods my cheeks. "Yeah."

"How old are you, babe?"

"Eighteen. I just turned eighteen last month."

"Oh, well thank fuck for that. Ain't I a dirty old man?" He laughs hard and I like the raspy, rumble that pours out of him a lot. Then he gives me a simmering look. "No wonder that fuckin' pussy of yours is so nice and tight."

I squirm under his coarse language, but he seems to like my discomfort. "Don't be shy, babe." His hand massages over my breast, rolling my nipple between his fingers. "These fat, pink nipples of yours are fuckin' perfect, babe. Everything about you is perfect."

I think if he keeps talking like that, my plans for revenge will go up in flames.

## Dante

SOMEWHERE, someone is looking down on me and smiling. One fine, fuckin' bitch I found today. I sure as fuck don't deserve her.

Eight-fucking-teen.

Jesus Christ.

"Stand up, babe."

She's so fuckin' sweet and eager. Doesn't ask why, just does it. Stands there waitin' for whatever I tell her next.

I slide to the edge of the bed and sit up. Her perfect tits are almost at my mouth, so I suck one nipple, lashing it with my tongue. I run my hand up her stomach. Grip her hips with my big hands. Nice, round hips, muscular thighs squeezing her little bush. Those fuckin' heavy tits, with fat pink nipples, that glow red when she's turned on. Flawless skin.

Goddamn.

"Turn around."

She spins without question, my hands sliding over all her smooth, silky skin. No ink. No birthmarks, moles. Nothing. Perfect, tight little ass.

I trace my finger down the length of her spine. "How does a pretty girl like you got no boyfriend?"

She shrugs.

I know, though. Fuckin' high school boys can't

appreciate what she's got. Woman's body too much to handle. But perfect for me.

I hook my arm around her and pull her into my lap, running my hand down her flat stomach. My fingers touch her pussy hair first. All soft and a little sticky from earlier. "Open," I whisper against her ear. A shiver works over her. Pink nipples standing straight, begging for my mouth. I shift my leg under hers, pushing her legs open, then slide my finger down, stopping to tease her clit, and then shoving it up inside her.

"Tight little cunt. You weren't no virgin, though."

"No."

My fucking cock throbs, needing inside her tight little hole, but I'm enjoying exploring her way too much to stop now, so I keep on fingering her. I tilt her to the side, and suck one of her nice, big nipples into my mouth while working a second finger inside of her. She's so wet, her juices drench my hand, making sloppy noises as I finger-fuck her. She moans and spreads her legs a little wider.

Her nipple pops out of my mouth with a nice wet sound. "You like that? Like gettin' fucked, babe?"

Her hand tightens on my shoulder.

"Answer me."

"Yes."

"How many boyfriends you had?"

Her body tenses at the question and I wonder about my new, little toy. There's something dirty about her, but also something real sweet and innocent.

"Two."

"They both fuck you?"

"No."

"When's the last time you got fucked before today?"

"More than a year." She's breathing so hard, she can barely answer, but she's so relaxed against me, hips rockin' in time to my fingers. Fucking perfect.

Her breath hitches and I move my thumb over her clit in tight circles. "Let go, babe. I wanna see you come for me."

"Okay," she breathes.

Sweet motherfuck. She's the hottest bitch I've ever seen.

"Come on, baby." I push and pull my fingers faster, rubbing her clit a little harder.

Her face pinches in concentration. "Yes, yes," she whispers, pulsing and throbbing around my fingers as she comes. Her hips buck wildly, chasing more.

"So good, baby. What a good girl. You come so pretty."

Her eyes slowly open and a soft smile turns her full red lips up. Her fingers reach out and caress the side of my face. "That was amazing. I've never. That's never—"

"You never made yourself come before, baby?"

She blushes and shakes her head. So shy for a girl I had laid out on the pool table not even an hour ago. That was a mistake on my part and ain't happening again. Not with this bitch. "Oh, we're gonna have a nice time. I'm gonna teach you all about how this hot little body works."

I shift her back onto the bed and crawl over her. "You on the pill?"

Her eyes go wide and she shakes her head. I got an urge to fuckin' slam into her anyway. But I also feel protective of this little one.

"We're gonna fix that. 'Cause I need to fuck you bare."

"Okay," she answers, all sweet and docile.

Fuck, I like this bitch. She's way too young and innocent for a twisted motherfucker like me, but fuck if I don't want to keep her anyway.

### Karina

"YOU LIKE SUCKIN' cock, babe?"

I nod even though it's not really true. I've done it because it's expected, but I can't say I really enjoy it.

"Hmm." Dante seems to see right through me.

He stands at the side of the bed. "Sit here," he says pointing to the edge, and I scoot over immediately. I stare up at him and he shakes his head.

"Fuckin' perfect," he grumbles.

He places a finger under my chin, lifting my face to look at him. He's a beautiful man. Big, muscled, strong. Dark hair covers his thick thighs. His cock stands tall and proud out from his body. I can't help but wrap my fingers around it. Or try to.

"Not yet. Don't be bad."

I snatch my hand back and he chuckles.

"I'm gonna teach you to please me. Forget anything else 'cept what I tell you."

"Okay."

He straddles my legs, tipping his hips to bring his cock forward. "Taste me. Get my dick nice and wet."

I glance up at him as I lick the head of his cock. "Don't be timid, baby. Lick it. From balls to slit." He guides my head down to his heavy sack, and I run my tongue along the thin skin, over the coarse hairs. He spreads his legs a little. "Rub up behind my balls, baby. Keep licking my nuts as you do it."

"Good girl. Now, put my dick in your mouth. Take me as deep as you can." I do. I want to satisfy him, so I take him until I gag. Above me, he groans, "Good, you're doing so good, baby. Again." I slide my lips back down and feel his hand at the back of my head. "Lil' faster, baby girl. Use your hands to stroke the base."

The slurping sounds I'm making should embarrass me, but they don't, because he seems to like them. I want to please him so badly that each time I suck him down deeper, even when I gag.

As if he reads my mind, he asks, "You want to please me, don't you, sweet girl?"

I nod, but don't stop.

He runs his hands through my hair. "Yeah, you do. You're doing a good job, too."

My lips smile around his cock and I push my tongue against him harder.

He groans, his fist tightening in my hair. "Look at me."

My eyes meet his, and he groans again. The lust in his deep brown eyes sends a rush of heat to my pussy. "Fuck, baby, I'm gonna come. You gonna swallow it all for me?"

I suck him harder, telling him without words, I'll accept anything he gives me.

"Yeah, fuck, suck it. Take it all." He groans loud and low as his cock pulses and spurts in my mouth. I gag and choke, but his hands hold my head steady. "Swallow it all like a good girl."

I do it, and he smiles down at me. "Fucking beautiful, girl, you know that?"

He wipes a drop of cum from the corner of my mouth and presses his finger against my lips. "Lick."

I make a show of licking the tip of his thumb and he groans.

"Fuck, I could go all goddamn night with you."

# CHAPTER TWO

**Karina**

"WHERE YOU GOING, BABY GIRL?" HE ASKS IN A SEXY morning-rough voice.

Shit. I was hoping to run out and be back before he woke up.

I'm still naked, but I have my dress in my hands. "I need to find the bathroom."

"Right across the hall." He points to his dresser. "Top drawer. Put one of my T-shirts on. Anyone says anything, you tell 'em you're here with Dante, got it?"

"Okay." I grab the first shirt my hand brushes against. It happens to be an Iron Bulls MC shirt. The hem hangs to my knees, so at least I'm covered, since I have no idea where my panties ended up.

I take extra time washing up. There's little in the way of soap or beauty products, but I make do with what I can find. As I step out of the bathroom, I'm so focused on Dante's door, I never see Logan coming at me. He grabs my elbow, tugs me down the hallway, and slams me up against the wall. His furious face is inches from mine.

"What. The. Fuck. Are you doing, Karina?"

"I, uh—"

"Does your father know you're here?"

I don't like being spoken to this way. My father hasn't been fatherly in years. Not since my mother died when I was twelve. When I needed him the most. He's out on the road most of the time and I fend for myself. None of this is Logan's business though. I stopped being his concern a while ago.

"Let go of me."

He loosens his grip, but doesn't let me go.

"Karina, you don't know what you're getting into with a guy like Dante. He's too old for you. Fuck, do you even understand what his role in the club is?"

"No. It doesn't matter though; he's nice to me."

"He fucked you in the middle of our living room and let me shove my cock down your throat. You call that nice?"

Heat burns my cheeks. "Leave me alone. You threw me away. I'm not yours to worry about anymore."

He ignores my accusation, but his eyes skip away from me for a moment. "You think you're gonna be hanging in my club, then you're my concern."

Something occurs to me. Logan can't have been a member for very long.

"Dante's above you, isn't he?"

Logan cocks his head at me. "So what?"

"You're jealous."

He snorts as if the idea is absurd. "I don't want to see you get hurt."

I force out some laughter of my own. "You're kidding, right? Let me go, or I'll yell for him. I bet you're not supposed to touch me without his permission."

He lets go of me in a dramatic gesture.

"Don't come cryin' to me when he hurts you, sugar."

"Don't worry. You're the last person I'd turn to."

I spin on my heel and hurry back to Dante's room. My hand's on the knob when I stop to take a quick look at Logan. He's eying me with pity and it ticks me off. I stick my tongue out at him and go back inside.

Dante's stretched out with his hands behind his head when I enter. His cock stands tall, tenting the thin sheet pulled over his body. My pussy throbs at the sight of him.

"What took you so long, baby girl?"

"I ran into Logan."

His eyebrows draw down for a brief second before understanding lights up his face. He's really fucking hot in an older, dangerous way. "Hemi? He bother you?"

"No."

"How you guys know each other?"

"He lived next door to me when we were younger."

That seems to satisfy his curiosity and I'm relieved he doesn't have any more questions about our past.

He holds out his hand to me. "You're lookin' fuckin' sexy in my shirt, babe. Come here."

I hurry over to the side of the bed, just out of reach of his fingertips. He quirks his lips at me and I wrap the hem of the shirt in my fingers and slowly slide it up my body. Giving him a little show is fun and he seems to like it.

"Fuckin' tease." But he says it with a smile.

When I finally ease the shirt off, he groans. "Get up here."

## Dante

CAN'T BELIEVE this hot little bitch is still here. Thought for sure she was making a run for it.

Fuckin' teasin' the hell out of me. Puttin' on the sexiest, but somehow sweetest, little strip show I've ever seen with my own fuckin' shirt.

I'm hard as a motherfuckin' rock.

"Get up here."

She places her tiny hand in mine and presses her knee into the bed. Her heavy tits sway just a bit and I can't help grabbing them, rubbing my thumbs over her fat, little red nipples. "Climb on top of me, babe."

She hesitates and seems unsure. I'm bettin' most of her experiences have been of the backseat of a car or sneakin' in a quickie before her parents come home variety.

"You ever been on top?"

She blushes, looking down at the bed, and shakes her head. Fuck, but she's sweet.

"You'll like it. Come on." I whip a condom out of the drawer next to the bed and roll it on while she watches and licks her lips.

"Did you want to suck that?"

She nods.

"Later. I wanna feel that tight cunt around my cock first."

I pull her on top of me and she goes right for my face, kissing my chin and up to my lips. Ain't never been with such a sweet girl. Soft and hesitant. I twine my fingers in her hair and tilt her head the way I want it, kissing her long and deep. My other hand slides down to grope her ass cheeks. She starts circling her hips and moaning, her hard nipples pressing into my chest. I tug her hair, pulling her back.

"Sit up."

She struggles a little, but pushes herself up, straddling my hips. My hands wrap around her tiny little waist and I lift her. "Grab my cock, babe." She hesitates, and I think it's because she doesn't want to touch the condom. Yeah, we're definitely gonna fix that shit today. She wraps her hand around the base of my dick and looks to me for further instruction.

Fuck, that's hot.

When she gets me to her opening, I grip her hips and thrust up into her, hard. She lets out a startled gasp and I wait a second for her to adjust.

"Fuck me nice, baby girl. Up and down. Slide all the way down. Take my cock."

Her teeth sink into her bottom lip and her eyes roll shut. Bitch is definitely diggin' this. I am too, because I got a prime view of her ripe tits and perfect body. Her tits are bouncing up and down just beggin' me to pinch and pull on them. The harder I tug on those little red beauties, the louder she moans. I bet she doesn't even realize she's gettin' off on the little bit of pain. I'm gonna be dreamin' about her fat, rosy nipples for months.

She's too wrapped up in what she's doing. Keeps grinding

down so hard on my dick, I have to struggle not to shoot my fuckin' load. I reach between us to stroke her clit with my thumb and she tosses her head back, moaning like a wild cat. She wants it real fuckin' bad, and I want her to have it. She grinds and circles her hips, but can't quite get what she's after. I rub faster circles around her clit, pinch her nipples a little harder, and she goes off. Screaming, whimpering, and crying as a hard orgasm rushes through her.

It's a beautiful fuckin' thing to see.

Her furious riding slows and her eyes pop open.

"Good?"

"Oh, yes," she answers in her little sex-kitten voice.

Fuck me.

I clamp my hands over her hips and lift her up.

"Hands and knees, babe."

Fuck, if she doesn't get right into position in the middle of the bed. Ass up in the air nice and high. Jesus Christ.

Positioning myself behind her, I run my cock through her ass crack. "Anyone ever fuck your ass, sweetheart?"

She trembles and turns to look at me over her shoulder. "No."

"Hmm." I want to take her ass, but I think it's something I'll ease her into another time. There's definitely going to be another time with this bitch. Can't remember the last time I wanted a bitch for more than one night. But this one? I can't envision a time I *won't* want to fuck her.

I slide my cock inside her pussy and watch as her head drops down. She lets out a long moan, as I work us into a steady rhythm. My hand slides over her ass again and she tenses up.

"Relax. I'll make you feel good."

She unclenches and I lean over to pull some lube out of the drawer. I spread her hot little ass cheeks and she flinches when the first drop of cold lube hits her asshole.

"Shhh."

She rocks back on my cock. Squeezes my dick so fucking hard. Trying to distract me with her tight little cunt muscles. So cute.

Using the tip of one finger, I massage the lube all around her hole until she relaxes. I slide that finger inside up to the first knuckle, working it in and out of her slowly, careful not to go too deep. When she relaxes, I start giving her my dick again. Working my dick in her pussy and my finger in her ass nice and steady.

Hoarse, strangled moans come from her throat. "Yeah, see, I told you it would feel good."

"Yes."

She's so fuckin' wet, juices dripping all over my cock and balls. I want her so fucking bad even though I'm already stuffing two of her holes.

I want to own this little bitch.

I start fucking her as fast as I can. Hips slamming into her, finger tunneling deeper into her clenching ass.

"Come for me, baby. Come with my finger in your ass, 'cause one day soon it's gonna be my cock."

She moans and trembles under me, then cries out. Muscles clamping down, juices gushing everywhere. She's shaking, but I keep hammering into her. The pressure building in my balls is intense and I let go, cum shooting out of me, filling the condom.

She collapses under me, and I follow her down. She turns and snuggles into me. Can't remember the last time I snuggled with a bitch. Guilt ain't something I've felt a lot of in my life. But I do feel a little guilty looking down at her. She's a soft, sweet girl who has no business with a man like me.

I want her anyway.

# CHAPTER THREE

### Karina

DANTE HAS ME IN HIS IRON GRIP. WITH ONE GLANCE at the clock, I start to freak out.

I need to get to school.

"Dante," I whisper.

He comes to right away with a scary look on his face. The expression softens when he takes me in.

"Damn, glad you're still here, baby. 'Fraid I dreamt you up."

Oh hell, that's nice to hear. "Nope. I'm real. But I need to get to school."

He hesitates, eying me up and down. I'm very aware of how naked I am and that he probably wants to fuck again.

"Please. I need to stop by my house, grab my stuff, and change."

After staring at me for another few seconds, he nods.

"Yeah, baby. You wanna eat somethin' first?"

"No time."

He shifts; one of his big hands settles on my face cupping my cheek and sliding down. His thumb strokes over my pulse. "Want you back in my bed tonight."

"Okay," I whisper.


## Dante

I HATE how much I hate letting this bitch out of my sight. I don't do relationships. I don't keep bitches around for more than a night or two.

She got on my bike behind me, wrappin' her arms tight around my waist. Her fingers curled into my belt like she never wanted to let go.

Before she got on, she gave me the address. I know her neighborhood. Slum area. The house she shares with her father is the nicest one on the block, but that ain't sayin' much.

It's deathly quiet, so the silence is deafening when I shut off my engine in her driveway.

She pries her little fingers from my belt and steadies herself on my shoulder to get off the bike.

"Thank you for the ride."

She makes my dick semi-hard actin' all polite and shit.

"No problem, babe."

I climb off, which seems to surprise her, but she doesn't say anything as she leads me into the house.

It ain't a total shithole inside. Even so, I can't help thinking my little bitch deserves better surroundings.

No, not my stank-ass bedroom at the clubhouse. My

actual home up in the mountains is nice, clean, comfortable, and quiet.

I don't ever take bitches there.

Worst part of all this is, for the fuckin' life of me, I can't remember this bitch's name.

While she wanders off—to, I assume, her bedroom—I take a better look around the house.

A note on the counter finally solves the mystery for me.

*Karina,*
*Be back Tuesday. There's money in the jar. Behave.*
*-Dad.*

*Karina.* I roll the name around on my tongue. Pretty name for a pretty girl. Tuesday, huh? It's Friday. I can have her to myself for two, whole fuckin' days this weekend.

My dick's rock-hard at the thought.

Her shoes tap over the cheap vinyl flooring as she walks into the kitchen. She lets out a startled gasp. "Oh, you're still here?"

"Yeah, babe. I didn't see a car in the driveway. You take the bus to school?"

"I usually walk."

"Why don't you have a car yet?"

She shrugs. "Can't afford it. My dad wants me to concentrate on school, so I only work during the summers."

Interesting. "You like school?"

She half-smiles. "Yeah."

Bitch is way too fuckin' pretty to worry about school and shit. Needs a man to take care of her.

*I want to be that man.*

She steps around me and pulls a yogurt out of the fridge. Doesn't look like much else inside. Her face turns pink. "I, uh, don't have a lot to offer—"

"I'm good, babe. Your dad leave you with any grocery money?"

She hesitates before answering. "I'm fine."

I don't agree, but I let it slide. What kind of man leaves his daughter with no food in the fuckin' house?

She tosses the yogurt in her backpack. "Well, I—"

"Yeah, let's go. I'm droppin' you off."

Shock stands out all over her face. "You are?"

Fuck me, but she's sweet. What was supposed to be an afternoon fuck seems to be turning into something else, and I don't know how to stop it.

"Yeah. You shouldn't be walking around here by yourself."

She seems surprised, but doesn't say anything as I lead her back outside.

Feels so fucking good with the girl tucked behind me, thighs cradling my hips, arms wrapped around my waist, and her cheek between my shoulders. I almost forget I'm dropping her off at school.

Damn, if I don't feel like a filthy pervert.

When I pull up at the student drop-off, she gets off and looks around all nervous-like.

"What's wrong, babe. Thought you didn't have a boyfriend?" I'm teasing 'cause some high school boy ain't on my give-a-fuck radar. But she scowls at me something fierce.

"No, I just don't want the principal to hassle you."

That's cute. Her thinking I give a fuck what some high school suit thinks about me.

"I ain't worried about it, babe."

Her eyes meet mine, and it's like staring into a bolt of lightning. A fuckin' jolt of lust rocks through me. "What time you done?"

Her eyes widen in surprise. *That's right, little girl.* Your man is gonna be droppin' you off and pickin' you up from now on. And when I got club business that takes me out of town, I'll make sure she's got a ride lined up. I don't tell her any of this though. One thing at a time.

"Two-thirty."

"Your dad coming home today?" I know he's not from readin' that note, but I want to see what her answer is.

"No," she practically whispers.

"When's he gettin' back?" Not that it matters. Girl is eighteen she can do what she wants. I might just have her tight little ass moved into my fuckin' house before her father rolls back into town.

"Tuesday, I think. He usually calls if he's gonna be earlier or later."

"Good. I'll take you by your house and you can pack some shit. You're staying with me this weekend."

"I am?" She ain't sayin' it to be difficult. She seems genuinely surprised I want her company for another night. Fuck, I'm surprised myself, so I can hardly hold it against the girl.

Reaching out, I run my thumb over her soft cheek. "Yeah, I got some club business today and I need to be at the clubhouse tonight; but tomorrow, I'll take you up to my house and we'll spend the weekend there."

Her cheeks flush and she can't seem to get any words out. Hooking my finger in the waistband of her jeans, I tug her close so I can whisper in her ear. "The only thing I need you to say is 'Yes, Dante.'"

"Yes, Dante," she whispers.

Holy motherfuck, those tasty nipples of hers are rock hard and on display under her flimsy little T-shirt. The way we're standing, I can look right down her shirt at the creamy swells of her breasts. It's takin' a lot of restraint not to bend her over my bike and fuck the living hell out of her here in broad daylight. "On second thought, we don't need to go to your house. You ain't gonna need any clothes this weekend."

Her face blushes an even deeper red. The bell rings interrupting our little moment.

"Go on. I'll be here at two-thirty."

"Okay." She leans in and presses a kiss to my cheek.

Sweetest motherfuckin' kiss I've ever gotten.

# CHAPTER FOUR

**Karina**

As I hurry into school, my mind is swirling with confusion.

I wanted to sleep with Dante to make Logan jealous. I didn't expect to wind up liking the guy so much.

Logan's warning still echoes in my head. What exactly does Dante do for the club?

My best friend, Athena, greets me with a knowing grin. "You look awfully smug today."

I don't meet her intense stare because I know I'll burst and we're already late for class.

"You can't hide shit from me girl. What were you up to?"

"I'll tell you at lunch! Let's get to class before Mr. Fitzsimmons has a stroke."

I like all my classes, but English with Mr. Fitzsimmons —or "Fitzy" as Athena and I call him during our gossip sessions—is my favorite.

He's fucking hot.

He's also the youngest teacher in our school full of relics.

Yesterday, I would have given my left tit to go home with him. Not that he ever gives any of the students a second glance. Word has it he's engaged to some stuck-up lawyer and is probably going to leave at the end of the year.

It's a shame because, besides being hot, he's a really good teacher. Something this shithole town desperately needs.

Today, I can't stop thinking of Dante. My face flames as I think of all the things I let him do to me yesterday, last night, and this morning.

"Karina? Are you paying attention?"

"Yes, Mr. Fitzsimmons."

Athena pokes me in the back and my hand automatically turns up for the note I know she's going to pass me. Using our cell phones to text each other during class is a bad idea with Fitzy.

**Athena: Michelle said she saw some biker drop you off. Was it Lucifer?**

That's our private nickname for Logan.

I give my head a subtle shake and get poked again.

"Athena, is there a problem?"

"No, Mr. Fitzsimmons."

English is the only class Athena and I share. We'll meet back up at lunchtime, where I know she's going to grill me.

Sure enough, she's waiting for me and yanks out a chair as I approach our regular table.

"Who's the guy?" she asks before my ass even hits the chair.

Oh, my God. How do I even describe Dante?

"He's in Logan's MC. He's their Sergeant-at-Arms. I don't know what that is, but I got the impression it's a big deal in the club."

Her nose wrinkles. "How old is he?"

I hadn't thought to ask. "I don't know. He's definitely older. He's so hot, Athena. And the best thing is Logan totally walked in on us."

"You screwed him?" she practically shouts. A bunch of people turn and look at us.

"Would you keep it down?"

"Sorry, sorry. I just worried that after Logan, you'd never...you know."

"Jeez, don't be so dramatic."

An announcement comes over the loudspeaker and the entire lunchroom goes silent. Turns out due to a water main break, we're being released two hours early. The cafeteria erupts in shouts and cheers.

I turn to Athena. "Think you can give me a ride?"

"Sure. Home?"

"Well, yeah, I want to pack a few things, but then drop me off at the clubhouse?"

"Are you serious?"

"Yeah, Dante wanted me to spend the weekend with him."

She nails me with one of her are-you-shitting-me stares. "Karina, your Dad will kill you."

"He's not going to know. He's away until next week."

"Any other hunky bikers I might like?"

Athena won't be eighteen until after graduation. Somehow, I don't think Dante would appreciate me bringing her into his clubhouse.

"Probably not, they're all older." I don't know this for a fact because the only other member I saw was Logan, but the surest way to get Athena to do something is to tell her she can't do it.

We go our separate ways, but meet up in the parking lot so she can drive me home.

At my house, I run in and toss some clothes into my backpack. I've got a few pieces of sexy underwear that I'd saved up for, and I add those in. Dashing into the bathroom, I take a quick shower, spending time shaving my legs 'til they're silky smooth. I don't bother with makeup, but I brush my hair and run the straightening iron over it until it's glossy and flowing down my back.

Then I throw on my shortest denim mini-skirt and a tight, red and blue plaid flannel shirt. I add short red cowgirl boots, snatch my backpack off the bed, and run out to Athena's car.

She bursts out laughing when she sees me.

"Wow, you've got it bad for this guy."

"Fuck off."

"No, you're hot."

The gate to the clubhouse is wide open, so Athena drives me right up to the door. A few younger guys are in the yard and they eye the car, but don't approach. The backs of their cuts read PROSPECT.

Athena takes my hand. "You're sure about this?"

"Yeah, he was really nice to me."

"What if he wants to watch the other guys fuck you one after the other?"

That sounds kind of hot, actually, but I don't want my best friend to think I'm a slut. "That's not going to happen."

"I don't want you to get hurt."

"Athena, I already spent the night with him. If he really wanted to hurt me, he had his chance. He drove me to school this morning."

Her mouth quirks up. "Hmm...a badass biker with a heart of gold. Nice story."

"You're nuts."

"Maybe. I want details Monday."

We kiss each other on the cheek and I get out. I run my hands down the sides of my skirt, and pull the backpack over one shoulder.

Entering the club alone feels odd, but I do it with my chin up and shoulders back.

I almost run outside after Athena's car when I spot Dante at the bar. He's talking to a busty blonde and from their posture it's clear they're familiar with each other.

So this was the business he had to take care of at the club today.

Dammit.

### Dante

Dropping my bitch off. Not being able to smell her, touch her, *fuck* her, isn't sittin' well with me. And fuck if that's not pissing me off. Once she's out of my sight, I start rethinkin' shit. Don't need a bitch. Ain't ever wanted one.

Just met this one yesterday. She's a hell of a fuck, but that's it. Why am I makin' more out of it?

The last fuckin' person I want to see is waitin' for me when I get back to the clubhouse. Fuckin' Hemi. It didn't escape my notice the way Karina went all weird talkin' about him. I'm guessing they were more than next-door neighbors and the thought of it is making me a little fuckin' nuts.

Hemi's a bit on the prissy side for a biker. How he got voted in is beyond me, even though I was sittin' at the table givin' my *yay* vote same as everyone else. He's a hard worker. Loyal to the club. Took a lotta bitch work as a prospect and never complained once. Handles shit good now too. He makes a point outta stayin' away from most of the club whores, which is why it shocked me a little that he was so willing to join in yesterday. Fuck, that's burning my balls now.

"I need a word, Dante."

"So spit it out. Ain't got time for bullshit today, Hemi."

"You done with Karina?"

Hell fuckin' no, he did not just go there.

I stop and level him with a look that usually means someone is about to get dead or beaten.

"And you're stickin' your nose in my sex life, why?"

I'll give the fucker credit, he doesn't back down. So he's either brave or real fuckin' stupid. Haven't determined which one yet.

"Look, I've known her since she was a kid. She's not like the girls you're used to. She's not some club whore."

"Let's ignore the obvious—which is I picked her up outside a coffee shop and had my tongue in her pussy not half an hour later—but, who I fuck is none of your goddamn business."

"If it was anyone else, trust me, I wouldn't care. But she's a smart girl. She's got plans to get out of this shit town and she doesn't belong hanging out here."

"You mean, with me."

"Fine. Yeah."

"*You* fuckin' her?"

"No."

"Before yesterday, when's the last time you saw her?"

"Almost two years."

"So, you might not know fuck about her anymore. Maybe her plans have changed. And maybe I don't give a shit what her plans are. She wants to leave town she can leave. I ain't stoppin' her." This might not actually be true, but it's none of Hemi's fuckin' business.

Hemi isn't going to be swayed off this conversation that easily. "She falls hard man. She's real smart. Last I knew, she was planning on medical school."

"What the fuck are you even talkin' about? You think she's gonna give something like that up for some one-night stand?"

"No. I'm thinking she's not able to handle a one-night stand; and since I ain't ever seen you with a woman for longer than a week, don't fuckin' break her heart. She should be concentrating on finals and college and shit like that."

I'm fightin' real hard not to punch the living fuck outta my "brother" right now.

"Are you her fuckin' guidance counselor now, too?"

"No. I was her friend for a long time."

"That all?"

He levels a fierce look at me. Kid's got balls of steel; I'll give him that. "No. I popped her cherry."

He says it like it's some sort of bombshell news, but I kind of already suspected this. "Thanks for breaking her in for me. She's a hell of a fuck."

Hemi gets a little red in the face and his fists ball up at his sides. This is rich.

"You seriously thinking about fighting your Sergeant-at-Arms over a piece of ass you ain't tapped in two years?"

"No," he spits out.

"'Cause I didn't get the impression you were the last guy up in her snug little cunt." This is actually a lie, but my goal ain't to defend her honor right now, it's to put this fucker in his place.

"Fuck you."

"No, thanks. We done here?"

"Yeah."

Little asshole storms off and I make a note to speak to our prez about Hemi's attitude. Normally, it'd be my job to discipline his insubordinate ass, but since we seem to have an issue, it should fall on someone else. I'll toss that problem in Prez's lap after church.

Speaking of—Prez steps out of chapel and whistles. His way of callin' all our asses in to sit down.

He slaps me on the back as I pass him. "'Sup, Dante?"

"Wanna speak to you after about somethin'."

"You got it."

Romeo's a fair president. Solid guy. Been leading our club for five years now. His name is a fuckin' joke. Never met a scarier motherfucker.

Besides myself, of course.

Brothers hustle to the table. We're outlaw bikers who live outside society's conventions, but we don't fuck around when it comes to our own rules. Everyone gets his ass to church on time.

Or else I beat the fuck outta them.

Just 'bout all our penalties for breakin' a rule involve a beatdown or payin' money into our common fund.

It's a good system.

Pain and money. Two things outlaws understand well.

We go through club business quickly. Someone's gotta take a run down to Mexico. This year I've done more than my fair share of runs. I got a lil' bitch I wanna spend some time with, so now I ain't goin' anywhere.

"Hemi ain't done a trip to Mexico yet. Send him and Viper down," I suggest.

Romeo glances at Hemi. "You up for it? Over the border can be tricky, but Viper knows the ropes."

Hemi glares at me. "Yeah, no problem."

Good. Fucker will be outta my face Wednesday. Lil' Karina and I might not still be a thing five days from now, but fuck if this kid is gonna get away with tryin' to tell me where to stick my dick. I'm the least of that girl's problems. At least I wanna help her out.

I realize I'm so fuckin' annoyed because if he's so damn concerned about her welfare, why the fuck ain't he takin' care of her? Why the fuck she walkin' through that bombed out ghetto to get to school every day? Why she livin' in a house with hardly any food in it?

Why is she so eager to pick up guys like me?

# CHAPTER FIVE

### Dante

THE REST OF CHURCH WENT BY QUICKLY. TWO hangarounds want to move up to prospects and it's up to me to do a background check. It can wait until next week. Nothing is going to stop me from spending this weekend balls deep in Karina.

I've earned it.

After the guys file out, Romeo lifts his chin at me.

Some of my anger has lessened. Especially now that Hemi will be out of my hair and with any luck rotting in a Mexican prison next week.

Don't worry; we've got connections to get him out. Although I like the idea of letting him sweat it out for a few days.

"I'm cool. Thought I might have an issue with Hemi, but I think we got it worked out."

"Okay. Think he'll survive this run?"

"Yeah." While he's an annoying little prick, he's smart. "He'll be fine," I add.

"Got plans this weekend?"

"Hell, yeah."

Romeo smirks at me.

The rest of the guys are prowling the clubhouse. It's still early in the afternoon so most of the regular club ass ain't here yet. But there's a few girls that are pretty much here round the clock to service the members. One of my favorites is also here. Sadie sits at the bar staring down at her cell phone. Probably waiting for me. I need to talk to her, but not for what she thinks.

I like Sadie. She sucks dick like a champ. All her holes are available anytime, anyway you want it, and with however many guys want to join in. She's pretty enough. Takes good care of herself. But there's something about her. Even if she showed up in a business suit, you'd never mistake her for anything other than a whore.

Which makes it all the more ironic that she's the receptionist at the local free clinic.

She brightens when she spots me and I throw myself onto the stool next to her. "How you doin', Sadie?"

"Better now, baby," she says while placing a hand on my thigh.

"Not today, girl."

She pouts, but she's a good girl who knows the rules. Her hand goes back to the bar.

"Can you do me a favor, sweet-Sadie?"

Her smile comes back at the endearment. "Anything, Dante."

"I need to get a girl into the clinic for the standard stuff."

Her mouth turns down at that. Sadie does not like competition.

"Yeah. When?"

"This afternoon?"

"Jeez, Dante. Even the pill takes like seven days before it's effective."

Huh. Good to know.

"Can you get her in or not?"

"Yeah. I'll text you with a time. That okay?"

"Yup." To keep her happy, I lean over and give her a peck on the cheek.

A soft voice whimpers next to me. "Dante?"

Karina. Fuck! Where the hell did she come from?

"Babe, what are you doing here?" I check my watch and it's nowhere near two-thirty, so at least I didn't fuck up. Her eyes dart between me and Sadie. What she's thinkin' is comin' through loud and clear.

Here's the fucked up thing. I've never given a shit what a chick thought. This same situation happened with any other of the hundreds of pieces of ass I've tapped over the years, I wouldn't give two fucks.

Now? I'm fuckin' worried I've upset Karina. I don't want to hurt her *feelings.*

What the fuck is wrong with me?

A nice, tight, young pussy is turning me into one pansy-assed motherfucker.

My hand shoots out, shackling her wrist and pulling her into my side. "Karina, this is Sadie, a friend of the club."

"Hi, Sadie," Karina says, while lifting her chin. Fierce yet polite, this bitch continues to amaze me. "I didn't realize you were *busy*, so I guess I'll go," Karina sasses me.

Squeezing her chin between my fingers, I turn her head to face me. "Watch. Your. Mouth."

I may be turning into a pansy over this chick, but I absolutely can *not* have her run her mouth at me in front of anyone associated with the club. If we were alone in my room, I wouldn't give a single, solitary fuck. In front of Sadie, no.

Her eyes meet mine, shiny with unshed tears and she blinks once. I let her go. "Sadie here works at the clinic and is going to get you an appointment for later today."

Every visible inch of Karina's skin flames pink. "Oh, ah, thank you. Are you a nurse?" she asks Sadie.

Sadie smiles softly, she seems to be taking a shine to Karina. Lucky me. "No, I'm a receptionist there. I just stopped by on my lunch break to see if any of the guys needed anything." She lifts her chin at me. "I'll text you later."

"Thanks."

Karina leans into me. "Are you going to go with me?" she asks in a quivery voice that gets my dick harder than steel.

Sadie's got ears like a friggin' bat. She catches my eye and shakes her head slightly. "They might not like that."

Fuck that shit. The club sends that goddamn clinic so much fuckin' business they should fly one of our flags. "She's the patient; it's up to her."

Sadie shrugs. "Whatever. Try not to fuck her before bringing her in."

If it's possible, Karina's skin turns even redder.

### Karina

"COME HERE, LIL' girl." Dante slides off the stool, takes my hand, and leads me to his bedroom.

"I, uh. I thought she said…"

"I want to talk to you in private."

That frightens me.

The forceful way Dante grabbed me and warned me not to mouth off to him before, both scares and excites me.

There's a small desk in his room, which I find funny. It's not like I picture Dante sitting down to write out checks to pay his bills or something. He pulls out the chair and nudges me over to the bed. "Sit," he orders.

I perch on the edge of the bed and he pulls the chair right in front of me and sits down.

"First. Why are you here now?"

"Water main break. They sent us home early."

He nods. "How'd you get here?"

"My best friend dropped me off."

"You wanted to see me that bad?"

Admitting it is hard. I have to look away. "Yeah."

His hand brushes my knee and I glance at him in time to watch him sweep his gaze over me as if noticing my outfit for the first time. His mouth quirks up in one corner. "You put that cute little outfit on for me?"

"Yes."

"Brought a bag all packed too, huh?" He nods to my backpack he'd dropped on the floor when we came in the room. Suddenly, I'm scared he's going to tell me I made a mistake and to get lost. That's the kind of luck I have with men.

"You said you wanted—"

"Oh, I want. Don't you worry, sweet thing. I want."

I breathe out a sigh of relief. I don't know why I care so much. Dante was supposed to be a one-off, so I could get even with Logan. But I actually like the guy.

"Couple things we need to get straight, though, Karina."

"O...Okay."

"One, don't ever sass me out there." He jabs a finger at the bedroom door. "In here, use that smart mouth all you want; out there, keep your attitude locked down."

I honestly don't know what to say to that. At some point, it dawns on me that my jaw is hanging open. He smirks a little, but continues his lecture.

"Two. I had a talk with Hemi earlier. He seemed awfully concerned about you for an ex."

This is news to me. Except for his outburst in the hallway this morning, I wouldn't have any reason to think Logan gave a shit about me. "What do you mean?"

He ignores my question. "You need to understand something. This club—we don't let bitches come between us."

I recoil at the way he says bitches. He means *me*.

"Don't get bent, babe. Shit like that can tear a lesser club apart. Not this one. What I'm sayin' is if you're available to more than one of us, you're available to all of us."

"But I'm not—you're the one—"

He takes my hand. "Calm down, babe, and let me finish. Normally, I don't give a shit. Sadie, the girl you met? Don't give a flying fuck who she spreads her legs for once I'm done with her, you understand?"

*Gross.* But I nod my head.

"I don't know why, but you're different—"

We're interrupted by the sound of his phone. He pulls it out and checks the screen. "Sadie says I can bring you over now and they'll fit you in."

I can't believe I'm relieved about going to the gynecologist. But I really want to get away from this whole Logan conversation, because I'm scared Dante's going to find out the truth about my motives for coming here yesterday.

Especially since I think my motives have changed.

# CHAPTER SIX

### Dante

MY GIRL'S BEEN QUIET SINCE OUR TALK. I'M ALMOST regrettin' being so harsh with her. But she's gotta understand, trying to play brother against brother won't end well for her.

As she dismounts from my bike—all flustered 'cause she's trying not to flash her pussy to the entire parking lot, with that tiny fuckin' skirt—she takes my hand. More from nerves than affection, I'm thinking.

Something occurs to me. "You ever done this before?"

"No," she whispers so softly, I almost don't hear her. Hell, this is awkward and I almost feel bad for pushing her into it.

Almost.

I can tell myself it's all about what's best for her. But I don't believe in lying. It's mostly about getting my bare dick inside her slick, tight pussy.

Sadie—cunt that she is—has also scheduled *me* for an STD screening.

"Very funny," I say with a hard stare.

She shrugs as if she doesn't see what the issue is.

Karina's big, innocent blue eyes blink up at me and something shifts in my chest. I've fucked around a *lot.*

"Yeah, fine," I grunt at Sadie. A smug smile curves her glossy lips as she taps some info into the computer and tells us to take a seat.

Karina gets called in first, and I get to wait like a perverted, douchey fuckwad by myself. When the waiting area is cleared of patients, Sadie takes a seat next to me.

"You really like this girl." It's a statement, not a question.

"I don't know. Why you askin'?"

She lifts her bony shoulders. "Known you a while now. Never seen you like this before."

I'm saved from whatever nonsense Sadie wants to reminisce about by the doc callin' my name out.

"Later, Sadie-girl."

The tests ain't anything I haven't done before. The lecture I get also isn't new. The fact that I actually pay attention to it is.

Karina's still not done when I go back into the waiting room. When she finally emerges, she's flushed and nervous lookin'.

I pay the bill Sadie hands me and take my little bitch home.

### Karina

Still mortified from the doctor's visit, I don't have much to say. It's a good thing we're riding Dante's bike to his house, because words won't be expected of me.

I'm shocked when we pull up to the serene log cabin up in the mountains. The grass is a little overgrown, but otherwise it has a well-cared-for appearance.

"Haven't been up here in a couple days," Dante explains as he helps me off the bike.

I take in the big Dodge pickup in the yard. "Grocery getter," he says, watching me.

Sure, that makes sense.

He takes my hand, leads me up the porch steps, and into the house. It's a little musty inside but otherwise neat and orderly. He walks through the house, throwing open curtains and pushing up windows.

"You can set your stuff down," he says, nodding at the couch.

I drop my backpack there and take in the living room.

Everything is nice, but sparsely furnished.

Dante stalks closer. When he reaches me, he takes my hands. "You're the first woman I've brought here."

That can't be right. He's obviously dicking me around. But as I look up into his eyes, I have my doubts. "Really?"

"Yeah, I told you—you're different."

"Why? You barely know me."

He squeezes my hands until I meet his gaze. "Don't know why. Don't care. There's somethin' special about you I like. A lot."

"I like you too," I whisper.

"Good. I gotta know though, there's nothing between you and Hemi anymore, right?"

"No. Not in a long time."

"Okay. You're in my bed and no one else's, understand?"

Heat shoots straight to my center. He wants me. Long term. That's what he's saying, right?

"Dante, that means you're only with me, then too. Right? That girl, Sadie—"

"Don't worry about Sadie. She's history. Your pussy's the one I want to be inside, baby."

How's it possible for him to be crude but sexy at the same time? Doesn't matter, I need to have an answer to my next question. "For how long?"

"Fuck, you're a pain in the ass," he says with a smile. "Long as we're still feelin' it."

That doesn't reassure me all that much.

"If you want...if you want someone else, you can tell me. Just don't lie to me, okay?"

Dante cocks his head to the side, his hands curl over my shoulders. "Someone do that to you?"

"Yeah. Just don't...don't hurt me, Dante."

"I won't, baby."

### Dante

I'm such a fuckin' asshole making promises to this little bitch, I know damn well I ain't gonna be able to keep.

*Faithful.* I don't know what that is.

*Freedom.* That's what my life's about. Riding when and where I want. Freedom to fuck any woman I want.

But the thought of some other guy with his hands on her, touching her, makes me motherfucking crazy.

Stupid as it sounds, I like this feeling. I don't want to let go of it.

The thought of some teenage asshole hurting her makes me want to murder.

"Dante?" she whispers.

Fuck, that sweet, tentative voice. Her quivering lower lip and innocent eyes.

"Yeah?" I answer in a hoarse voice.

"What do you want to do?"

I'm so caught up thinkin' about her, even though she's right in front of me, that we're just standing in my living room staring at each other.

Like some lovesick douche, I hold my hand out to her and she takes it. "Let me give you a tour."

Her pretty lips twitch into a smile.

And I actually give her a tour of the small cabin I built with my own hands and help from my brothers at the club.

"Can you cook, babe?" I ask her when we step into the kitchen.

"Yes," she answers while blushing furiously.

"Wanna cook for me?"

She glances at me as if I'm fuckin' playin' a joke on her. "Sure, if you want me to."

"Later." I tug her past the small downstairs bathroom and up the stairs to the second floor. It's surprising that I've never brought a woman here, because it's all set up like some fuckin' love nest.

The second floor is a master bedroom and a bathroom. Got a nice, fancy Jacuzzi tub that I'm lookin' forward to getting Karina in.

Hell, I just want any excuse to get her naked.

A slight tremble works over her as she stands staring at my bed.

Fuck, I want her more than I've ever wanted anything else.

So, I take her.

Yank her up against me.

Kiss her harder than I've ever kissed a woman.

Strip off her soft flannel shirt.

She shimmies out of her skirt and is left standing in her little cowgirl boots and some sexy, red scraps of lace.

Taking a step back, so I can admire her, my hand rubs over my chin and down my chest. "Fuck, me."

She hesitates and fixes her gaze on the floor.

"Look at me, Karina."

She snaps her head up.

"Turn."

Fuck me. All see-through fucking lace underwear. Sweet, round little ass cheeks peeking out.

I can't stand another second of not touching her, so I take the last few steps, and mold myself against her back. My hands cup her tits; I rub my thumbs over those juicy nipples I can't wait to get in my mouth.

"Ohhh," she moans, as she sags against me. Fuck, that's nice.

Every reaction I get from this little bitch is the real thing. No fake shit from her. Don't think she could fake it if she wanted to.

"Go get on the bed."

"Okay," she whispers.

As she steps up to the bed, she turns to me. "How?"

At first, I think she's askin' me how to get on the bed,

and I'm concerned about her intelligence. Then, I realize she's asking how I want her to position herself on my bed.

Jesus.

Christ.

My mouth's so fuckin' dry. My dick's harder than it's ever been.

My filthy mind flips through a bunch of scenarios.

"Get in the middle, babe. I'll be right back."

I've never had a woman here, but that doesn't mean I haven't always assumed one would find her way here eventually. I've got condoms, toys, and some other stuff stashed in my bathroom, so that's where I head.

The site that greets me when I return is fuckin' cute as hell.

Cute. What the fuck is happening to me?

Karina sitting Indian style in the middle of my bed. Just waiting.

For me.

Her eyes go all round when she sees my hands full.

I set everything on the dresser and strip my clothes off. I could live off the way her eyes drink me in. Soakin' me up like I'm the sexiest man she's ever seen. Makes all the time I spend workin' out worth it.

As soon as I pull my briefs down, she crawls over to the side of the bed and reaches out to stroke my cock. I'm so fucking hard and aching for her already. I don't get a chance to say anything before she's opening her mouth and sucking on my dick. Cute little ass tipped in the air, hands and mouth stroking and licking.

Little bitch remembers everything I taught her.

*Goddamn.*

My hands reach out to stroke over her firm ass. Rubbing her smooth skin and rough lace.

*Crack!*

My hand leaves a nice little pink imprint on her juicy ass.

I expected her to jump. Cry out. Stop sucking my dick. But she moans around my cock and sucks me down harder.

So I spank her ass again.

And get the same reaction. Except she wiggles her ass further into the air.

Begging for my hand.

So I give it to her. Careful to catch the nice, round fleshy parts of her ass.

Christ, she's suckin' me down so hard, my eyes roll back in my head. White lightning streaks down my spine. My fuckin' balls tighten and before I can even warn her, I'm shootin' a huge fuckin' load down her throat. She licks and sucks every last bit of my cum. Moaning and humming away.

"Fuuuuck, baby. You're my good little cocksucker, aren't you?"

She finally lets me go, and sits back on her heels, placing her hands in her lap.

"Was that okay?"

"Better than okay. Remembered everything I taught you, yeah?"

Pink stains her cheeks and she looks down at her hands. "I tried."

I can't help reaching out to run my finger over her cheek until she meets my gaze. "Good girl."

Fuck. I'm so fuckin' far beyond turned on by her.

"You like it when I spank your ass?"

She shrugs and looks away.

"Look at me, Karina. Answer me."

"I guess so."

"Anyone ever do that to you before?"

"No."

I want to do it to her.

And realize there's no reason I can't.

She's fucking *mine*.

Sitting next to her on the bed, I reach out and curve my arm around her little body. She immediately curls against me, which is sweet, but not what I'm after.

As I continue to exert pressure on her back, she tenses. "What do you want me to do, Dante?" she asks in her sweet, hesitant voice.

"Over my lap, little girl."

Her jaw drops, but her eyes light up. She melts into a puddle over my lap. Perfect ass positioned right where I can rub my big hands over her firm round cheeks. With my other hand, I grab the material of her panties, pulling it tight between her cheeks.

"You've got a perfect ass, Karina."

"Thank you," she says.

Hooking a thumb into the waistband of her underwear, I order her, "Lift up."

She raises her hips for me to tug her panties down her legs, leaving them around her knees. Fuckin' fantastic ass. Smooth, round, and firm. Tight, young flesh. Posed and waiting so perfectly. Waiting for whatever I want to do to her.

I'm a bastard. I know I am. One sick motherfucker when I want to be. Here my girl is, so naïve. I'm fuckin' thankful she ran into me, and not someone worse who'd hurt and misuse her. She's much too trusting.

It makes me want to protect her.

*And* punish her.

Raising my hand, I bring my palm down on her ass with a satisfying crack. She flinches and I take a second to admire the handprint I left on her ass cheek.

My other arm clamps across her waist to keep her anchored to my lap.

She quivers against me, waiting for the next blow. I don't give her a lot of time to think it over. Just swat her and enjoy watching her ass turn red. She moans and wriggles, but doesn't yell or try to get away.

I'm already fucking hard again.

My palm stings, so I stop and admire her glowing ass. She raises her hips a bit, as if begging me to keep going.

Unreal.

I rub her ass in small circles, then trail my fingers down to her thighs. "Open."

She parts her legs and I work my hand over her pussy.

"Soaking wet, little girl. Someone likes bein' spanked."

Moans and sighs are the only answer I get from her.

So fuckin' slick, I work one finger into her tight little pussy, enjoyin' the way she squeezes my finger tight. Fuck. I need to be up inside her right the fuck now.

# CHAPTER SEVEN

### Karina

FACE DOWN OVER DANTE'S LAP, I'VE NEVER FELT safer or happier. Each spank leaves me hot and aching for his cock. The next slap makes me moan, a begging, needy sound. My skin flushes hot that I sound so desperate.

His big hand stroking my ass, his finger pushing inside, I'm so ready.

"Need to fuck you, Karina."

"Yes, please."

He groans at my answer, and my world spins as he shifts me off his lap and onto the bed.

Reaching over me to the nightstand, he plucks a condom out of an open box and rips it open.

"They told me—"

"I know. It's fine, baby girl."

*Baby girl.* Oh my God, I love the way he calls me that.

I gasp as he slides his thick, muscled arms under my

thighs, spreading me wide for his cock. He pauses before sinking into me.

"Fuuuck, baby girl, you're so fuckin' tight."

"You're just so fucking big," I answer, surprising myself.

He roars with laughter and takes my mouth in a demanding kiss. Time spins away as I lose myself in all the pleasurable sensations spiraling through me. His cock sliding in slow, stretching me. He works into a pattern, stroking over that magical spot inside of me that feels so good. Our tongues, licking and crashing against each other. His rough hands squeezing and stroking my breasts, thumbing my nipples.

My orgasm washes over me, warm and sweet. Before I know what's happening, Dante slides out of me, snaps off the condom, and shoots hot cum all over my tits and belly.

Eyes half-closed and sexy lips turned into a smirk, he looks extremely satisfied with himself. But I think I know what will please him even more.

I run my fingers through the sticky wetness, rubbing his cum into my skin. Over my breasts.

"Pinch your nipples," he breathes out.

I do and he groans.

"Let's get you clean."

He slides his arms under my body and carries me into the bathroom. I don't know what to think, except I like the way he makes me feel. Dirty, used, protected, and cherished.

Nuzzling my forehead against his stubbly cheek, I ask the question that's been burning in my head all day. "How old are you, Dante?"

His gaze flicks down, searching my face. "Thirty-four."

"That's not that old," I answer as he sets me down next to the tub.

He lets out a big, booming laugh. "No?"

"No. Logan said you were too old for me, but I think you're just right."

His jaw twitches and I wish I'd kept my mouth shut. "When'd he say that?"

"This morning when he grabbed me outside the bathroom." Whoops. Too late, I realize I should have chosen my words more carefully.

His eyes narrow. "Whaddya mean, grabbed you?"

My shoulders jump up and down. "I told you—"

He turns and flips the shower on, waiting for it to heat up. "Yeah, but you didn't say he put his hands on you."

"I'm sorry."

He nails me with another hard stare. "Don't be sorry. Not your fault. He shouldn't be touching what doesn't belong to him. I'll need to make that clear when he gets back from his run."

I let out the breath I didn't realize I'd been holding.

"What?" he asks, studying my face.

"How long will he be gone?"

"Should be less than a week."

"Oh."

He laughs again. "Were you hoping for longer?"

"Maybe."

He grunts and takes my hand, leading me under the hot spray. I squeal and turn away. "Hot! Hot!"

He pushes me behind him and adjusts the

temperature. "Sorry, babe. Forgot you got all that soft, silky skin. Not a tough rhino-hide like mine."

It's such a silly thing to say, I end up giggling. When the water cools, he spins us around and washes me clean. His strokes turn from simple cleansing, to dirty teasing fast. "I loved seeing my cum dripping off these fat nipples, baby."

I squirm in his grasp as he rolls and pinches my nipples. "Did you just call me fat?" I pant out.

Leaning over, he nips at my neck and shoulder, pinching my stiff nubs even harder. "No, I called these juicy, sexy-as-fuck, little nipples fat. Don't start that shit with me, babe. You're fuckin' perfect. Already told you. Showed you." His hand smacks my wet ass cheek, and I groan.

When I'm cleaned to his satisfaction, he turns us again and hands me a washcloth.

"Clean me up now, lil' girl."

"Yes, daddy," I whisper, and then freeze. What the hell made me say that? Embarrassed, I stare at our feet.

He places a finger under my chin, tipping my head up. "You call your father that?"

"No, never."

He nods once. Eyes narrowed. Expression hard, making me shiver. "Wash me then, baby girl," he orders.

My mind races as I soap up the cloth and run it over his firm muscles. Every now and then, I stop to inspect some random scar. One I'm pretty sure is a bullet wound. Two that look like he was stabbed. The Iron Bulls MC tat takes up his entire chest and is an impressive piece. He's got full-sleeve tattoos, vibrant and colorful. I can't get enough of his abs or the sexy V leading down to his semi-hard cock. But I can't stop thinking about the words that popped out of my mouth either.

Christ, am I so starved for attention, I'm turning into some needy woman with daddy issues?

Duh, of course I am. Otherwise, I wouldn't be picking up guys on the sidewalk for a marathon sex session. Letting him take me to the clinic. Spending the weekend at his house.

Calling him *Daddy*.

## Dante

*YES, daddy.*

*What. The. Fuck.*

Lust slams right the fuck through me. Never, *ever* have I wanted a bitch to call me *that*. Some have tried and been rudely corrected. It always seemed wrong.

It's *not* wrong when it comes out of Karina's mouth.

It's right.

Except for one thing. "You call your father that?" I ask her.

"No, never."

She washes every inch of me thoroughly and appreciatively. I'm rock hard and ready to fuck her again in no time. This is insane.

When we're all clean, I shut the water off and lead her out. Little shivers work over her, so I wrap her in a towel and dry her off. She balances holding on to my shoulders while I pat down her legs. Her stomach growls as I lean over.

"You hungry, baby girl?"

"Yeah. I haven't eaten since lunch."

Well, of course she hasn't. She's had my dick in her all damn day.

Taking her by the hand back into my bedroom, I toss her a T-shirt. "You bring some jeans?"

"Yeah."

"Get dressed, I'm gonna take you out."

She pulls another sexy fucking pair of tiny panties out of her backpack and I have to turn around or she's gonna pass out from starvation when I fuck her again.

Knowing how cool the mountain air will be on my bike, I toss her a sweatshirt before we head downstairs.

Riding always clears my fucked up head. It gives me clarity and peace of mind that nothing else can. Not weed, booze, or pussy.

Right now, the thing I'm fucked up about has her arms wrapped tightly around my middle. Her small hands resting right above my dick. Tight little body pressed up against me. Juicy thighs hugging my hips.

I'm aware of every move she makes. When her arms tighten around me and I sense she's scared, I slow the bike down. Never worried about shit like that before.

We ride for a while. I don't want to end up someplace we'll run into any of my brothers. I don't leave our territory either. It's just better that way. I'm wearin' my cut and she's wearing my sweatshirt with my club's logo.

I like the way she looks in my clothes.

The pizza place I pull up to is a family-type joint,

complete with red and white plastic tablecloths. I lead her by the hand to a table in the back and seat her with her back to the rest of the room. I put my back to the wall so I can see any potential threat and take care of it before my girl gets hurt.

That's just how my mind works.

The menu is one page. But Karina studies it for a while before glancing up.

"What do you want on your pizza?"

"The garden one sounds really good."

Awful thing to do to pizza, but I nod. When the waitress comes, I do the ordering.

"One of those antipasto salads to split. Large pizza, half carnivore, half garden." The waitress quirks her mouth at me.

"Drinks?"

I glance at Karina and she addresses the waitress. "Root beer, please."

"Just bring us a pitcher, thanks." I hand her the menus and she leaves.

I'm fascinated by the woman across from me. Back at my cabin, she's all needy little girl. Doin' what I ask, looking to me for instruction. Out here, she's fully in charge of herself.

It's a huge fuckin' turn-on.

That's why I needed to get us out of the house. In public. A place where I can't just stick my dick in her every second.

Taking one of her small hands in mine, I trace my finger over the fine blue veins visible through her pale skin. "So, Hemi said you want to be a doctor?"

She tries to jerk her hand out of my grasp. "He told you that?"

"Yeah. Says you're real smart."

Her face screws up with confusion. "Really?"

I'm uncomfortable with where this is going. She seems a little *too* excited hearing what Hemi thinks of her.

The waitress drops off our salad, soda, and two plates.

Karina seems fascinated by the pinwheels of meat and cheese on top of the salad. She plucks one off the top with her fingers and nibbles on it before heaping forkfuls of salad onto her plate.

We eat in silence for a while.

"Good?" I ask her.

"Mmhmm," she hums, sounding pleased.

The waitress sets up a folding metal tray stand next to the table.

"Pizza's comin' better finish up," I tease her. When the fuck did I turn into a guy who jokes around with a woman?

She grins at me as she sets her fork down. "I love this place."

"You've never been?"

"Nope."

The waitress carries out our pizza. I take the cutter from her and dish out slices for each of us. Karina picks up her fork and knife, cutting her slice into smaller pieces she then picks up with her fingers. It's the oddest thing, but also somehow endearing.

"I don't want to be a doctor anymore," she says after a while.

"No?"

She shakes her head. "Too much school. Too much money. Long hours. I'm thinking more like an X-ray tech or something I can finish quickly, but still make money."

"You do well in school?" Like the asshole I am, all I'm thinking 'bout is the fact that the club could use someone with medical knowledge to help us out when things get rough.

She shrugs. "I always want to do better, you know?"

No, I really didn't know. I hadn't given a fuck about school, other than getting out, but I nod anyway.

"So, what does your father do that he leaves you alone for so long?"

She twitches and shifts in her chair before answering. "He's a long-haul trucker."

Something pricks at the back of my mind. Club's got a trucker who runs some shit for us to Santa Fe every couple weeks.

"Where's your mother?"

"Dead."

Shit. "Sorry, baby girl."

She shrugs and glances away. "Happened a while ago."

"What else do you like to do?"

She flicks her eyes up at me, as if she's surprised I give a shit. Hell, I'm surprised myself, so I can't blame her.

"I read a lot. Hang out with my friend Athena. Nothing exciting." Her lips curl up into a sexy smirk. "Well, until yesterday when this sexy biker picked me up."

After her earlier behavior, this more forward, seductive thing she's doing is fuckin' hot. I'm really likin' how unpredictable my little bitch is.

"You stayin' with me the whole weekend?"

The vixen is replaced with something more vulnerable. "If you want me to."

"Yeah, I want you to." Hell, I'm ready to move her into my cabin permanently. Right the fuck now. But I'll see how the weekend goes and tell her on Sunday.

Then she says three words that make my dick rock hard the instant they leave her lips.

"Then I'm all yours."

# CHAPTER EIGHT

**Karina**

DANTE STOPS AT A GROCERY STORE ON THE WAY back to his house. "Ain't got much food back at the cabin, babe."

Not a lot of room with the bike to bring groceries back either. We purchase enough supplies to carry us through breakfast and lunch tomorrow.

We make it back to his cabin right as a rainstorm hits. It's crazy because we haven't had rain in I don't know how long. But the sky cracks open and we're soaked before we make it to the front door.

I squeal, hating the feel of my wet clothes sticking to me. Dante and I tumble into the kitchen, where I help him put the groceries away. We're both dripping water all over the floor, when he turns to me with one eyebrow raised.

"Strip."

"Wha-what?" My voice quivers at the unexpected request.

Dante leans back on the counter and folds his thick arms over his chest. "You heard me, baby girl," he answers in that low, commanding voice that turns me to jelly.

"Yes, daddy."

I yank the sweatshirt he let me borrow up and over my head and set it on the nearest counter. Next, my T-shirt. I shake wet strands of hair out of my eyes, before reaching for the button on my jeans.

"Turn around and peel those jeans down nice and slow."

More heat curls in my belly. My nipples are painfully hard and it has nothing to do with the chill.

Slowly, I turn, arching my back and peering over my shoulder as I undo the button and work my pants over my hips. Behind me, Dante groans.

"That's it, baby girl. Nice and slow."

I wiggle and tease him a little before slipping my jeans under my ass. Bending over and swaying gets a louder groan from him, so I work the material off faster. Unfortunately, everything gets tangled up in my boots and I almost tip over.

How clumsy and embarrassing.

I sob, on the verge of tears.

Then Dante's hands are on my hips. "Stuck, little girl?"

I nod pitifully and he turns me to face him. His mouth crashes over mine, taking me in a rough kiss. Big hands wrap around my waist, carrying me to the counter and setting me down. At first, I think it's to help me get my shoes off, but Dante has other ideas.

"I kind of like you all bound up like this. Lie back."

I don't even think about it before cool counter kisses my bare shoulder blades.

"Stretch your arms over your head. Yeah, nice."

He uses my jeans as a sort of handle and lifts my legs in the air, while he frees his cock. "Stay," he orders me, while he whips out a condom and rolls it down his thick shaft.

I don't move a muscle.

He doesn't just slam into me though. Lightly touching me, he smiles. "All wet and ready for me, baby girl?"

A full-bodied shiver rips through me. My breath rushing in and out in quick puffs. Dante just keeps on smiling. Stroking me, circling my clit with his wet, rough fingers, until I'm quivering and trembling at every touch. I'm burning with the need. But I also enjoy the way he's playing with me, teasing me.

"Tell me you want it," he demands.

"Yes, please, I want your cock so much," I plead. My girly bits are throbbing with so much need I don't have the decency to care about how desperate and pathetic I sounded. I just want him inside me, relieving this agonizing ache he's stirred up.

He doesn't laugh, or tease me for my desperation. If anything, his expression intensifies.

"Yeah, my baby girl wants it bad."

I nod frantically. "Yes."

His cock prods my entrance, but he doesn't slam into me. He thrusts gently, nudging himself inside me inch by thick inch, while leaning over, staring down at me. Watching my every reaction. Another drag of his cock out and back in. Stretching me open, filling me, the friction of his cock against my sensitive skin shooting sparks of pleasure all over me. I roll my hips, arch my back to invite him deeper. When he seems satisfied I'm ready, he moves fast and wild, pounding into me over and over. The counter is slick with our sweat, and I slide a little. Dante pauses, fumbling with my shoes, ripping my jeans off my legs. He cups his hand over my shoulder, holding me in place for his punishing thrusts. I wrap my legs around his waist and hang on.

It doesn't take long for his cock to bring me right to the edge. Hot shivers work down my body as I reach my peak. I scream out words that make no sense, my body jerking from the orgasm tearing through me.

Above me he shudders, opens his mouth and lets out a harsh shout. But his eyes never leave my face. His arms shake, the cords in his neck stand out, but he keeps pounding his hips wringing every last bit of pleasure from both of us.

When he finishes, he lowers his head, touches my mouth with his. This is different from our earlier encounters. It's tender and grateful and wonderful.

### Dante

As our heart rates slow, I'm slammed with one thought.

I'm fucked.

I'm so motherfucking fucked.

*This girl.*

My longtime cold, bitter heart is shattering and disintegrating. In its place is something alive, warm, and pulsing with need to possess *this girl.*

I can't afford to be warm in my life. Anything that belongs to me can be used against me.

The thought of anyone harming her has me ready to dismember men with my bare hands. This isn't just some weekend fuckfest. I know this. I'm already planning to move her into my goddamn house for fuck's sake.

"You okay, baby girl?"

Those beautiful pink lips curve into a soft smile. "Yes. I'm more than okay."

Fuck, she's sweet. I don't want to pull out of her, but my softening cock and soggy condom say it's time. I toss the condom in the trash and clean up. Holding my hand out to her, I pull her into a sitting position and help her off the counter.

She stares up at me with a cute, awed expression. "My legs are shaking."

I can't help laughing. "Mine too, babe."

Stalking over to the sink, I pull down two glasses, fill one with water, and hand it to her. She gulps it down in greedy pulls and sets the glass on the counter. As I take a few sips from my own glass, her gaze bounces around the room. As if on autopilot, she starts picking up our discarded clothes.

"Leave it."

"But—"

"Leave. It."

She sets the clothes in her hand on the counter. "Okay."

Taking her hand, I lead her upstairs and we get ready for bed. The lights are off and I'm under the covers for a few minutes when she slides next to me. Even in the dark,

I sense her hesitation. Lifting my arm out, I beckon her to me. "Come on, baby girl."

She nudges and nuzzles her way under my arm, throwing her leg over mine, wrapping her arm around my waist and after a few minutes falls asleep.

The rest of the weekend is pretty much the same. We fuck. We talk. Karina cooks for us. She's a hell of a cook, making me want her even more.

Sunday night we're in the living room. I'm on the couch. She's sitting on the floor between my feet doing her homework.

Yeah, it's weird. But I keep reminding myself she's eighteen.

Every now and then I reach out and run my fingers over her hair and she hums or leans back against me. Other than that, she's very focused on her work.

When she finishes, she stuffs her books and notes into her backpack. "Do you have a computer I can use?"

"Not here, babe."

She chews on her bottom lip. "I should have brought my laptop."

"What's wrong?"

"I need to submit an essay to one of my teachers."

"Can you do it in the morning?"

More lip chewing. I press my thumb against her chin to get her to stop. "Yeah," she finally answers.

I pat the cushion, inviting her to sit next to me. A playful-smile flickers over her lips.

"I want to talk to you seriously."

Her teasing smile disappears replaced by nervous lip

biting. Once she's sittin' beside me, I take her hand. "I like you a lot, Karina. Want you to move in here."

"What?"

"Did I stutter? I want you here. Like havin' you around. Like your cooking. Love fuckin' you. I *don't* like you living in that neighborhood by yourself all the time. Or walking to school through that neighborhood by yourself."

"But I need to get to school."

"I'll take care of it."

"My father—"

"Your father lets you fend for yourself. He's gone long stretches." I reach out and trace her cheekbone with my finger, sliding down to cup her chin. "Baby girl needs to be looked after."

Those are the magic words. A hiss of air rushes through her parted lips, her pupils dilate. Next to me, her body trembles like crazy.

"Yes," she finally whispers. "I'd like to be here with you."

"Ain't gonna lie to you, sweetheart, there's times I'll be out on a run and not here for long stretches. But if you're here I won't be takin' as many runs for the club as I do now." I'm fuckin' plannin' to make Hemi take as many runs as possible. Keep that asshat far the fuck away from my little bitch.

"Okay." She hesitates. "Dante? What about school? In the fall, I'm planning to go to State, live on campus…"

I shrug. "Campus is what? Forty-five minutes away? I'll come see you or you'll come home."

Relief spreads across her face. "Oh, okay."

"I ain't gonna stop you from goin' to school, babe.

Besides, this might not work out." I hate sayin' it, but it's the truth.

Her face falls.

"Babe, come on. You might get to campus and decide an old fuck like me ain't worth wasting your time on."

Her lip quivers and she shakes her head. "I don't think so."

# CHAPTER NINE

### Karina

BY TUESDAY AFTERNOON, I'M ALL MOVED INTO Dante's place. It's not like I had a lot of stuff to bring. But there was enough to fill half of the bed of his truck. I leave a brief note for my father letting him know I've moved out and give him the number of the cell phone Dante pressed into my palm when he picked me up from school.

That was the first of the surprises. The second was waiting for me at his house.

"A car?"

"Yeah, babe. There's gonna be days when I got club business and can't take you to school."

"But—"

"It's nothin' fancy. But it will get you to school and back. In the fall, it will get you to college and home to visit me on the weekend."

The last part he says low and growly against my ear. My legs are like jelly, barely able to hold me up.

"Dante, I need to tell you something." Shit. Why didn't I do this *before* I packed all my stuff into the back of his truck?

"By that look on your face I ain't gonna like this, am I?"

I close my eyes and say the words in a rush. "Thursday when we met, I, uh, knew who you were. I wanted to hook up with you to make Logan jealous."

With his big hand guiding my shoulders, he turns me. He snorts, "Look at me."

The anger I expected to find on his face isn't there. "You still feelin' Hemi?"

"No."

"Wantin' to make him jealous—sounds like you're still hung up on him."

"Not anymore."

"'Cause you're feelin' me?"

"Yes."

He blows out a breath and stares somewhere above my head before meeting my eyes again. "Look, I ain't gonna lie and say that doesn't piss me off. But I was plannin' to fuck you and send you on your way, so I ain't got much room to talk. My plans have changed since then."

"Mine, too."

He nods once. "Okay. You need to listen up though. Once I announce you're my girl in front of the club, that's it. Hemi comes near you, shut him down. He'd be fuckin' stupid to try. I won't tolerate my girl jumpin' beds. You fuck him after you been fuckin' me, you're off my bike, out of my bed, and if you still want to hang at the clubhouse, you're club ass available to any brother. Understand?"

"Y-yes."

"Good."

"You still want me to move in?"

"Fuck yeah, babe."

"You're not mad at me?"

He doesn't say anything and I squirm while I wait. "No. I ain't exactly thrilled, but I respect you for tellin' me. Now, I think the way you're going to make it up to me is by suckin' my dick and makin' me dinner."

My mouth twitches into a grin. "I can do that."

### Dante

*DAMN FUCKIN' right.*

Karina works off her guilt by gettin' on her knees and suckin' me off like her life depends on it.

At first, I was pissed.

Then I was amused.

Karma is gettin' even with me for all the fuckin' women I've used, discarded, fucked, and forgotten about. It's downright fuckin' funny that the one bitch I actually want to keep, was using me to get even with her ex.

I think we'll be fine now. Long as Hemi stays the fuck outta my business. Think I'll have her up to the clubhouse Friday and introduce her around. Not as my ol' lady. Fuck that shit. But as the girl, who is off limits to those horny motherfuckers.

Holding her head the way I need it, I push my cock all the way to the back of her throat. She gags a little, but keeps her mouth nice and wide. "Good girl. You're gonna swallow everything I give you."

She whimpers a little, but it only cranks me up more. One more thrust out, then in and I'm coming so hard I can barely see straight. She sucks and licks every last drop then rests her head on my thigh when she's finished. My hand brushes her hair off her face, taking in her flushed cheeks and unfocused eyes. "Good girl," I praise her. She responds by wriggling closer to me.

"You got homework, baby girl?"

"Just a little."

"It's gettin' late. Why don't you start on that, and I'll make us some sandwiches for dinner."

"But. You said you wanted me to do the cook—"

"I know what I said, baby girl. Changed my mind. Get to work."

I tuck my cock away and kiss the top of her head before standing. The whole house is an open floor plan, so I'm able to watch her while I put dinner together. It doesn't take me very long before I'm calling her to come sit at the counter.

"Come eat. Then you can finish your work."

"Okay."

Christ, the way she all but fuckin' glides across the living room is sexy as fuck. She's got no fuckin' clue either. Graceful as a cat, she perches on one of the barstools and picks up her sandwich. Love a woman who has an appetite and I've yet to see her turn down food.

"Hey, you got one of those little plaid skirts?"

She quirks an eyebrow at me. "You mean like a schoolgirl type thing?"

"Yeah."

"I think so. Why?"

"Want you to wear it for me Friday when I take you up to the clubhouse."

Her eyes widen, cheeks flush, but her bottom lip trembling is what gets my attention.

"What's wrong?"

"Nothing."

It fuckin' dawns on me what she's worried about. "I ain't takin' you up there to share you with anyone, babe. The opposite, actually. Want my brothers to know if they see you at the clubhouse, you're off limits." Especially fuckin' Hemi.

But I keep *that* to myself.

# CHAPTER TEN

### Karina

FRIDAY NIGHT I FIND MYSELF DRESSED UP LIKE something out of an old Britney Spears video. When I told Dante I didn't think I had everything I needed to complete the outfit, he handed me a wad of cash and told me to go shopping.

So I did.

Athena found all of it very amusing.

My father left me some angry voicemails during the week I haven't bothered to return yet. Dante left Wednesday night on what he said was a "short run," so he asked me to meet him at the clubhouse tonight, since he had to go straight there when he returned. Before he left he made sure I was thoroughly fucked and that the refrigerator was stocked.

"I can't believe you moved in with some biker thug," Athena squawks at me. This is probably the hundredth time this week she's expressed her disbelief. We're standing in the parking lot after school and I cast a glance around to make sure we're not being overheard.

"He's not a thug."

She slants an are-you-kidding-face at me.

"Well, he's not to *me*."

She thrusts her chin up at my car. "Yeah, I guess so." She reaches out and hugs me. "I'm glad you're over Logan for good."

"Me too." I realize I mean it, too. Dante has obliterated everything and everyone else from my mind. And probably my heart.

"Okay, go have fun getting fucked fifty ways sideways," she chirps with a wave.

"What the hell does that even mean?" I grumble to myself as I get into my car.

Flipping down my visor, I brush my hair free of tangles and weave it into two thick braids. Dante didn't specify anything other than the skirt, but I have a feeling he'll appreciate my attention to detail.

Next to me, my phone peeps and I scoop it off the seat.

**Dante:** *Where's my baby girl?*

Good Lord, this man makes me wet with a fucking *text*.

**Me:** *School parking lot. Leaving now.*

I wait to see if he responds. When he doesn't, I put the car in gear and head to the clubhouse.

The parking lot is full of big, black, shiny motorcycles, huge pickup trucks, and a few cars. It's only three in the afternoon, but that doesn't seem to matter. This MC apparently likes to get the party started early. Afraid of going in alone with so many people around, I send Dante a text saying I'm outside before I get out of my car.

Apprehension swirls in my belly as my heels click over the pavement. Dante said he didn't want to share me. But during the week, I'd picked up a bit of gossip about the sort of things that went on behind the big black doors of the Iron Bulls MC.

A kid I recognize from my high school rushes over. He's wearing a plain leather cut. His lone patch reads "Prospect". My face heats up under the scrutiny of his blatant stare. The sweater I'm wearing is tight, and the V shows a hint of my boobs, but my belly is covered. My skirt is an actual skirt. It's short, but my ass isn't peeking out or anything. There's definitely a few inches of bare leg between my knee socks and the hem of my skirt, though.

"Who're you here for, sexy thing?" he asks while still running his horny gaze over me.

"She's mine," Dante growls from the doorway.

The prospect's face twists into an *I just shit myself* expression and I have to slap my hand over my mouth so I don't laugh.

"Hey, baby girl," Dante calls to me, his warm rough voice slides over my skin, leaving goosebumps.

"Hi," I answer shyly. I'm not sure why. He's been away for the last two days, so I guess I'm unsure if we go right back to the way things were before he left.

Instead of calling me over to him, he steps outside. "Get lost," he barks at the prospect, who takes off around the corner.

As he stalks toward me, he lifts his chin. "What's wrong?"

"Nothing."

When he reaches me, he settles his hands on my hips and looks me over. He hums an appreciative noise. One hand reaches up to toy with my braids. "You went all out for me, didn't you?"

Overwhelmed by the butterflies he stirs up inside me, I can only whisper, "Yes, daddy."

"Fuck, baby girl. I fuckin' missed you."

"Missed you, too."

"You ain't actin' like it."

"I'm sorry."

"Don't be sorry; give me a fuckin' kiss."

Laughter bubbles up out of me as I stretch up on my tiptoes to throw my arms around his neck. He picks me up, pressing me tight against his front. Our lips crash together. My mouth opens the second his tongue touches my lips and he strokes inside. Liquid fire flows straight to my core. We stay like that for a while, kissing, licking, groaning into each other's mouths.

Behind us someone clears his throat. "Romeo's lookin' for you, bro."

Dante releases me and I slowly slide down his body until my feet hit solid ground. He's got a healthy erection straining the front of his jeans that I'd love to take care of for him.

"Thanks, Wolf. I'll be right there." His eyes never leave my face.

He waits until the door closes before saying anything.

"Romeo's our Prez. Keep quiet unless I tell you it's okay and then keep it short and polite."

I should be offended by that, shouldn't I? I'm not though, because I'm terrified of meeting the rest of the Iron Bulls MC. Their reputation in this area is well known and downright frightening.

And I'm willingly walking into their clubhouse dressed like something out of porno.

### Dante

I'M A SICK MOTHERFUCKER. Karina's fear of entering the packed clubhouse is obvious, yet it's turning me on something fierce.

As I reach out to wrap my fingers around the door handle, she squeezes my hand, tugging me backward.

"Dante, what should I call you?"

Interesting question.

Moving her away from the door, I cup her cheek as I consider my answer.

"Dante."

She nods and tries to pull away from me, but I stop her with a hand on her shoulder. "Hey." I lean over and whisper in her ear, "Fucking love when we're alone and you call me daddy, baby girl. But that's our thing we share. Don't like my brothers in my business. Not with you."

"Oh. Okay."

"Now come on, Prez don't like to be kept waitin'." I curl my arm over her shoulders and guide her inside.

Inside is something out of a bad seventies porn—

maybe three cocks away from a full-blown orgy. Next to me, Karina presses herself into my body so tight she's practically up inside me.

Romeo's at the bar, so I point us in that direction. I take the stool next to him and have Karina perch her hot little ass on my lap. Takes me a minute to realize she has her backpack with her, as she slips it off and sets it on the floor.

Romeo shakes his head at me. "You bringing school girls into my club now?" Since I've known him for fuckin' ever, I can tell he's joking. Karina doesn't know, so she clings to me even tighter.

Romeo leers at her and gives her a wolfish grin. "How old are you, sugar?" Karina's big, blue eyes blink up at me and I nod.

"Eighteen," she answers.

"Yeah?"

He thrusts his chin at me. "You check her I.D.?"

"She's fuckin' legal. Stop being a dick. She's living up at the cabin with me."

Romeo raises an eyebrow, as the significance of that sinks in. He knows damn well I never bring bitches to my home.

"Gonna show her the chapel?"

Am I gonna claim her as my ol' lady? Lay her out on the big, oak table with our Iron Bulls MC logo carved in the middle, and fuck her in front of every one of my brothers?

"Fuck no," I answer. From behind the bar, Luck hands me a beer and I take a deep swallow. "Well, not tonight anyway," I amend. Sometime in the future, yeah I'll probably do a proper claiming and slap a property patch on her back. Missed my little bitch the entire time I was away from her.

That earns me another raised eyebrow from Romeo.

"What'd you need to talk to me about?" I ask, letting my fingers graze the bare skin of my girl's thigh. She shivers against me and I struggle not to bend her over the bar, flip her skirt up, and fuck her in front of everyone.

"Hemi. He did fuckin' good."

Too bad, I was hopin' he'd get himself into some trouble. "That's good."

Karina hasn't moved a muscle. Didn't even twitch when Hemi's name was mentioned. She's focused on the open space in front of her. Brothers takin' bitches every which way. Right out in the open.

"Baby girl, you want somethin' to drink?"

She blinks and smiles up at me. "Yes, please." Aw fuck. That little please makes my dick twitch.

"Luck, you got a root beer back there?"

Romeo snorts, but I don't give a fuck, because Karina's smiling at me for remembering what she likes.

Luck hands me a bottle and I pass it to her. Romeo watches her take a pull from the bottle and set it down. He shakes his head.

"You got any reports for me?"

I glance at Karina. She don't need to hear any of this shit.

"Baby girl, why don't you go put your backpack in my room." It's not really a question or a suggestion and I pull out my room key as I'm sayin' it.

She bends over and then seems to remember she's

wearing that little skirt in a club full of bikers, and squats down the rest of the way to snatch her bag off the floor. I press the key into her hand and look her in the eye. "Anyone bothers you, tell 'em you're Dante's girl. Anyone touches you—" I tap my chest right over my Sergeant-at-Arms patch, "memorize what their patch says and come tell me."

"Yes, Dante," she answers all sweet and docile.

The second she turns the corner and Romeo bursts out laughing. "You motherfucker. How the fuck you pull a piece of ass like that?"

"Watch it," I growl.

Luck leans his thick arms on the bar. Fucker's built like a tree and almost as big as me. I ever get taken out of commission, he's the one I'd pick to fill my job.

"She's submissive," he says low enough that only I hear him.

"No shit."

"No, I mean she's a natural submissive."

Romeo misses nothing, as usual. "Yeah, I bet you could order her to get on her knees and suck all our cocks in the middle of the room and she'd do it without hesitatin'."

Nothing about that idea appeals to me. "No. I ain't doin' that to her."

"Why the fuck not? She's a hot little bitch. Don't be greedy."

Luck slants a bordering-on-disrespectful look at our president. "Naw man," he jerks his head in the direction where Karina disappeared. "Submission like that is a gift. You don't fuckin' abuse it." He glances at me and points at my patch. "Bet she doesn't even know what that means."

My head tilts to the side in agreement.

He waves his hand at the rest of the room. "She ain't one of these club whores lookin' to hook up with an officer in the club. She ain't gonna ride every cock in here hopin' someone takes her as an ol' lady. She's with you 'cause she likes you."

Maybe that's not exactly how we started out, what with her childish revenge plot against Hemi, but he's right. Karina and I fit together like two pieces of some fucked up puzzle and I ain't offerin' her up to any of my brothers again. I'm still fuckin' livid with myself for lettin' Hemi near her.

"She ain't up for grabs, Prez. I'm serious."

He holds his hands up. "All right, all right. Fuck, never seen you so gone over a bitch before."

I shrug. "First time for everything."

# CHAPTER ELEVEN

**Karina**

DANTE'S ROOM IS EASY ENOUGH TO FIND.

So is trouble.

Trouble comes in the form of two barely dressed women who spot me leaving Dante's room and follow me.

Dante assumed I'd be harassed by one of the guys. Guess it never occurred to him it would be one of his club girls who hassled me.

"Where the fuck did you come from?" The tall blonde one sneers at me.

"I'm with Dante," I answer as nicely as possible.

"Yeah, we figured that, you comin' outta his room and all. But who the fuck are you?"

As they're talking to me, they're also sort of pressing me up against the wall. I'm trying to be as polite as possible, hoping it diffuses the situation, but it doesn't seem to be working.

"Fuck off," Logan shouts at them from the end of the hallway.

Both of them jump and pale when they see how furious he is.

"Shit! Where did you come from?" the short, chubby redhead squeaks.

His boots thunder down the hallway as he approaches.

"Get the fuck away from her."

"What are you doing here, sprite?" he asks after they scurry away.

*Sprite.* Is he kidding me? He hasn't called me that since we were kids and I decided that was the only thing I would drink for an entire summer. Even after I grew out of that phase, the name stuck. Until—

"Karina? What are you doing here?"

Shaking my memories from the past away, I lift my gaze to his face. He seems concerned. Happy to see me almost.

"I'm here with Dante."

His face hardens. What? Did he think I was here looking for him?

"You can't be serious." He runs his hand through his hair. "Fuck, that's why he sent me off on that run, isn't it?" he mumbles. I don't think he's looking for an answer from me, so I don't give him one.

"I need to get back. Thank you for rescuing me." Before he has a chance to say anything, I pivot and make my way back to Dante.

He's sliding off his stool when I enter the room. The serious expression on his face changes when he sees me.

"I was just gonna come lookin' for you."

"Um, two of your girls were bothering me. Logan... Hemi, chased them away for me."

His face contorts into anger and I step back. Lightning quick, his hand reaches out, curling around my bicep, pulling me to him.

"You okay?" he asks.

The tension inside me releases when I realize he's not angry with me. My head bobs up and down.

"Who?"

"I don't know their names. A short, chubby redhead and a tall, skinny blonde."

He nods once and scans the room. I follow his gaze, but don't see either of them. He grunts. "I'll deal with them later. You tell 'em you were with me?"

"Yeah, they didn't seem to care."

His jaw ticks. "Okay. Hemi say anything to you?"

My gaze drops to the floor. "Just asked me what I was doing here. I told him I was with you."

Rough fingers tickle under my chin, lifting my head up. "What did he say?"

"He seemed surprised."

That seems to satisfy Dante and he leads me back to the bar. Planting himself on the same barstool, this time he pulls me between his legs, with my back to the bar. Between his body and the lip of the bar, I'm sort of protected from view. That turns out to be a good thing, because Dante's fingers trail up my bare legs, under my skirt. His big hands grasp my thighs, and then skim to my ass.

He leans forward and whispers against my ear, "You're wearing panties?" His hot breath fanning over my neck sends a shiver straight to my nipples. Placing my lips against his ear, I whisper back, "Yes, daddy."

He groans. His thumbs hook into the string at my hips and tug downward. His dark eyes pin me in their lustful hold. "Take them off," he orders.

Even though I'm nervous about all the people in the room, I don't look away. I shimmy my hips a little and he guides the material down my legs. When he reaches my knees, I bend and take them off the rest of the way. He snatches them out of my hand, stuffing them in his back pocket.

"Better."

His gaze sweeps over me, heating my skin. With the bar at my back and his strong legs squeezing my hips, I'm caged in place. One corner of his mouth lifts in a devious smile and I wonder what I'm in for.

"Give me that pussy, baby girl," he orders in a low, rumbling voice.

As if my body belongs to Dante, my hips tilt forward and my thighs spread. He works his hand between my legs, sliding over my bare pussy. "Mmmm...someone was busy while I was gone."

A soft moan leaves my lips and my head drops forward. "Yes."

"You let someone touch my pussy?" he asks.

He's still stroking over my outer lips. Teasing and exciting me. "No...no. I shaved it myself."

He makes a low growly noise of approval, and my pussy throbs in response. "You do that for me?"

"Yes," I whisper.

"Tell me," he demands.

Confused, my eyebrows draw down and my eyes search his face for answers. Taking mercy on me, he leans in. "Say 'yes, daddy, I shaved my pussy for you."

A groan tears out of me as one thick finger prods my entrance. "Yes, daddy, I shaved my pussy just for you," I repeat back in a rush.

As soon as the words are out, he slides his middle finger inside me. The palm of his hand grinds over my clit and I gasp.

"Yeah, that's my good girl. Your hot, tight little cunt is dripping." Slowly he pumps his finger in and out of me.

"You want another finger?" he asks.

I can't form any words, so I just shake my head.

"Yeah, you do." He pulls out and pushes two fingers into my slick channel.

I gasp; my hands fly to his shoulders, digging in so I don't collapse on the floor.

"Open your eyes, baby girl. Otherwise everyone's gonna know I'm finger-fucking you."

It's not easy, but I manage to open my eyes. Dante's serious face is almost enough to make me come on the spot. My body relaxes when I glance around the room and realize no one is paying any attention to us. My juices are flowing freely; my thighs are damp and slick.

"You're so fucking hot. I couldn't even look at another woman while I was away. Can't stand bein' near any female that ain't you." His voice is raw as he admits this and his words push me closer to the edge. Knowing the effect I have on this older, experienced, and extremely sexy man goes straight to my head.

I wiggle my hips. "That's right. Ride my fuckin' fingers. Come on my hand."

"I...I...can't," I gasp.

His thumb flicks over my clit and my hips jerk forward. "Yeah, you can. Do what you're told."

My hips rock in time to his thrusting fingers. Letting out a deep, shuddering moan as I come, I fall against his chest. He wraps his arm around me. His other hand slides out from between my legs and reaches around to cup my ass cheek. Lightly, his fingers trace the seam of my ass.

"I want this ass, baby girl," he murmurs against my ear.

The idea of him taking me there scares me and I whimper. His hand slides down my back to cup my other ass cheek. I nuzzle into him harder while he squeezes and plays with my ass.

"That was fucking hot," a voice says behind me.

Harsh laughter rumbles through Dante's chest, jostling me away from him. My eyes open and I find him genuinely laughing. "Fucker," he mutters. The guy throws him a towel, which Dante uses to wipe his hand, and my cheeks heat up. "Got sweet girl cum all over me," he says with a laugh, making me blush harder.

Dante turns me, but I can't meet the eyes of the guy behind the bar. "Don't worry, sugar. I couldn't see a thing," he says gently. His words unlock me and I'm able to glance up. He's a hard, scary man. Almost as big as Dante. He smiles at me and it turns him into a handsome man. I can't help smiling back.

"This is Luck. Luck, this is my girl, Karina."

"Hi," I mumble, which makes the other guy laugh.

"She's a shy one."

Dante chuckles. "Yeah."

"Brother, can I have a word with you?" Shame washes over me. I don't need to look to know who it is, but I do anyway.

*Hemi.*

### Dante

The way my little bitch catches fire for me is something else. Even though I know she's nervous in a room full of people, the second I slid my finger in her tight snatch, everyone else in the room disappeared for her.

And fuck me; but knowing sometime while I was away, she shaved that sweet little pussy while thinking about me? Makes all the club ass I turned down on my run worth it.

I'm so fuckin' hard I don't know if I'll be able to walk to my room. If I don't get my dick inside her tight heat very soon, I'll lose my motherfuckin' mind.

Just as I have Karina 'bout to come on my hand, Luck strolled up behind her. He's on the other side of the bar, so I don't really care if he watches. Can't see much anyway. He raises an eyebrow at me and I lift my chin. She's a lot louder than I think she realizes and Luck smothers a smile.

The way she gets all embarrassed when she realizes what he overheard, even turns me on. Fuck, she's cute.

My good mood is interrupted by the last motherfucker I feel like talking to right now.

"Brother, can I have a word with you?" Hemi asks from my side. He's standing way too close to my girl for my taste. I glare at him, but he stays rooted to his spot. Kid has fuckin' balls; I'll give him that.

"What?" I snap.

He glances at Karina, who seems to be trying to ignore Hemi by keeping her eyes on me. I like that a whole fuckin' lot.

My arm tightens around her waist, and my hand smoothes down her backside, making sure she's covered. I don't want this little prick seeing any more of her than he needs to.

"Alone?" he asks.

"Club business?"

Again, his gaze darts to my girl. No, this ain't about club business, that's clear. He's gonna try stickin' his nose in *my* business, again.

This shit is gonna end now.

He meets my eyes with a challenging stare. "No."

"Then you can say it in front of *my girl*."

To the best of my knowledge, the kid ain't dumb. He knows damn well what that means.

He straightens up and looks at me. "Why is she here again?"

Behind the bar, Luck whistles low. Karina twitches against me and I hug her tighter.

Luck snaps his fingers in front of Hemi's face. "You might want to rethink this, brother."

Hemi acts like he didn't hear or see a thing. Karina's arm snakes around my waist, holding on to me tight. As if I'd kick her out on Hemi's say-so.

"I already know about your past relationship. That's it —*past*. You don't want to start this war with me."

Hemi's eyes widen in shock. "Since when are you with a bitch for more than a fuckin' day?"

Karina flinches. Now, maybe in *my* head I think of her affectionately as my little bitch. But Hemi callin' her that?

No. Hell fucking no.

Nudging Karina upright, I lift my chin at Luck. "Will you watch her?"

He glances at Hemi and shakes his head. "Yeah, no problem."

"Let's step outside, brother." I say to Hemi.

Motherfucker *still* doesn't have the sense to back the fuck down. It makes me wonder if I'm losing my edge or if the kid has lost his fuckin' mind.

Clamping my hand down on the back of his neck, I lead him out the door.

It's almost dark, but there's still enough daylight for what I need to do. Two prospects milling around outside glance over and I jerk my head toward the clubhouse. "Go inside."

I'll give Hemi credit he stands and faces me like a man. No begging or pleading.

"You know I'm within my rights to beat the shit out of you, right?"

He doesn't give an inch. "She shouldn't be here, man."

My fist flies, hitting him square in the jaw. I don't put my full force behind the blow, but he still rocks back on his feet. "She's with me," I growl.

He staggers back, rubbing his hand over his jaw. "Her dad know she's hanging with you?"

"Ain't none of your fuckin' business, you little shit, but she's all moved in with me. Don't give a fuck what her father thinks. She's eight-fucking-teen and can make up her own damn mind."

Hemi sucks in a breath, his nostrils flare, and his fists flex at his sides. "That why you sent me on the Mexi-run?"

"No. It's about fuckin' time you start pullin' your weight 'round here."

He grinds his teeth. "I almost didn't make it back over the border."

"Well, then I guess you'll have to be more careful next time."

One of the front doors swings open and Romeo steps out. "Everything good, brother?" he asks me.

"I don't know. Are we done havin' this conversation?" I ask Hemi.

"Yeah, whatever. If she wants to ruin her life, I don't give a fuck anymore."

A savage growl rips out of me and I lunge at him. Romeo lets me get in a few good punches before he pulls me off the kid.

"What the fuck, Hemi?" he shouts down at the kid, who is now on the ground. "You disrespectin' a brother over some piece of ass?"

"Watch it, Prez."

Romeo glances at me and smirks.

Hemi glares up at us and goes to stand. I step to him, fists raised. "Stay the fuck down, asshole."

"She ain't some piece of ass, Prez," Hemi mutters.

"She with you?" Romeo asks.

Hemi's chin drops to his chest and he shakes his head from side to side. "She was."

I snarl at him. "Ancient history, you little fuck."

Romeo holds a hand up. "Way I see it, Hemi, she wants to be with Dante. She's legal. No one forced her in here. You need to drop this or we're gonna have problems."

All the defiance seems to drain out of Hemi. He nods once. "Yeah, okay. Message received."

He pulls himself off the ground and extends his hand to me. "Sorry, brother."

The last fuckin' thing I want to do is shake his hand. But with Prez watching over us, I do it.

Romeo nods his approval. "Good." He claps Hemi on the back. "Come on. You should be celebrating. Did good this week, kid. Plenty of unattached bitches inside."

"Yeah, okay."

Something about the way Hemi says it makes me think he's not okay with any of this.

# CHAPTER TWELVE

**Karina**

LUCK'S A NICE GUY, WHO TRIES TO ENTERTAIN ME while Dante and Logan are outside.

Why is Logan suddenly so concerned about me? After the brutal way he broke my heart, I can't say I'm not thrilled over how much my relationship with Dante seems to bother him.

I'm also thrilled that I don't feel a damn thing for him anymore. How can I with Dante in my life? Big, tough, domineering Dante, who makes me feel safe and protected. Logan's no match.

Romeo, the president, stops by the bar.

"Where'd your man go, sweetheart?"

Luck answers for me. "Had to take Hemi outside for a talk."

Romeo raises an eyebrow. "No shit. 'Bout what?"

Luck tilts his head in my direction. "Hemi seems to think he's got some claim on Dante's girl."

"Your cunt lined in gold, sugar?"

My gasp of surprise at his crude question makes Romeo snicker. He pushes away from the bar. "I better go check on 'em before Dante kills the little punk."

It never occurred to me Hemi was in any real danger. I feel a little bad, even though it's not my fault Hemi interfered.

Luck plants his elbows on the bar and leans forward. "Wanna tell me why Hemi was willing to risk a beatdown from our Sergeant-at-Arms over you?"

Shaking my head, I can't come up with any answer that makes sense. "What's a Sergeant-at-Arms?" I ask.

He drops his head and chuckles. When he finishes, he glances up. "He enforces the rules of our club. Makes sure brothers follow club policies, and expected models of conduct when dealing with fellow brothers. Being that Hemi directly disrespected Dante, someone else should probably discipline him." He shrugs. "Dante won't kill him."

"God, I hope not." I mean, I hate Logan for how he treated me, but I don't want to see him beaten to death either.

Luck tries to keep me from worrying by telling me stories about the club and different runs he and Dante have gone on together. Nothing in-depth or serious. More like funny anecdotes.

Our attention is drawn to the door. Romeo stalks in first, followed by Dante and Logan. I gasp when I take in his bloody lip and the bruises already forming on his face.

He follows Romeo and doesn't even glance in my direction. Dante watches him for a minute before heading toward me. When he reaches me, he leans over and seals his mouth over mine, melding our lips together. His tongue licks at my bottom lip and I open for him. Our kiss deepens as he places his hands on either side of my face, holding me still.

I'm on fire by the time Dante pulls away. My eyelids flutter open to find Dante smiling down at me. "Much better now," he remarks.

My tongue swipes across my lips, tasting every lingering bit of him.

"You showed restraint, brother," Luck says behind us.

Embarrassment burns over my face. Once again, Dante managed to make me forget there are other people all around us.

Curling his hands over my shoulders, Dante turns me to face the bar and Luck. His big warm body presses up against my back making me feel safe and protected again.

"Took a chat with my fists and Prez for him to see the light. Fucker's stubborn."

He doesn't even look at me while talking about Logan and I can't decide if that's good or bad.

While he and Luck chat, Dante's hands absently massage my neck and shoulders. It feels amazing and I let out a soft moan, my head falling back against his chest. "Tired, baby girl?"

"No." I want to be alone with him, and not to sleep.

A few more people come up to talk to Dante. He introduces me to each one as "his girl," which thrills me each time he says it. There are so many new faces and strange road names that I can't memorize them all. Something I tell Dante when the last guy walks away.

He smiles at me. "That's okay, baby girl. Long as they know you're mine."

His, damn I like that.

Leaning down, his lips brush against my ear. "I've got a present for you in my room."

"Oh, really?" Somehow, I don't think he's serious. I'm pretty sure the present is his cock, and I'm totally fine with that.

The possessive way his hands circle my upper arms to help me off the stool, kicks up a throb of desire in my belly.

Dante nods at Luck. "You got this?"

Luck answers with one of those chin jerks men do that speaks volumes.

Dante's big hand closes around mine and leads me down the hall. I'm trembling with need before he opens the door and pushes me inside. The slam of the door makes me jump, but he doesn't notice. He's too busy pushing me up against the door.

Holding me tight against the solid wood, he leans down and takes my mouth in a savage kiss. Every thought leaves me, except for how this hard, rough, demanding man has the softest, fullest lips. He keeps me backed against the door, pressing his hard body against me.

My hands clutch at his leather cut, the wild beat of his heart drumming against my hand. He presses our kiss deeper, tongue sliding against mine, taking me. I want to slow things down and savor every bit, but at the same time, I want him to strip me bare, bend me over, and fuck me until I scream.

He backs away slowly, finishing our kiss, brushing his lips against mine, touching his forehead to mine.

"I hate how much I missed you," he says as if he really is angry about it.

That hurts. "Why?"

"Because if something ever happened, anyone tried to take you from me, I'd fuckin' murder them. You're worth killing for."

I don't get to respond. His mouth touches mine and I surrender completely. His arm wraps around my waist as he keeps tasting me. Claiming me.

Both of his hands slide down to cup my ass, lifting me.

"Dante," I moan, breaking our kiss.

"Yes, baby girl?"

"I need you," I gasp, lifting my legs and hooking them 'round his waist opening my body to him, so my bare pussy rubs over his denim-covered cock. His fingers find and run over my smooth, sensitive skin. He seems fascinated with my grooming choice and I'm so happy I decided to do that for him.

His mouth moves to my neck, the journey is rough and expresses how much he wants me. My man runs the pad of one finger back and forth, higher and lower until he hits the spot that makes me gasp. For such a rough man, he brushes against my sensitive clit gently. I'm so close, I buck my hips and he chuckles against my neck. His fingers move back to my soaked opening, pushing inside.

"Oh, Dante...so good. But I need your cock."

"Say please."

"Please, daddy, can I have your cock?"

He growls and presses his hips into me, keeping me

pinned to the door. Somehow he holds me up while freeing his cock and lining it up with my entrance. "You still taking your pill?"

"Every morning,"

He taps the fat head of his cock against my bare pussy lips, then whips out a condom and rolls it down his thick shaft. "Just in case," he mutters.

I don't have time to be insulted, because he pushes inside my body and groans. "Fuck, baby girl. You feel so fucking good. Didn't even think about fucking another pussy while I was gone. Only thought about yours."

With the frantic way we're grinding and thrusting against each other, I'm amazed he got so many words out. I pick up each one and even though they're crude, I absorb the warmth behind them.

I tighten around his cock and he groans louder, slams into me harder. My ravenous need for him destroys everything else.

"So fucking perfect," he groans. His mouth stops moving, and crushes against mine again. This is how Dante communicates best.

"Come for me, baby girl. Come around my cock. Show me you missed me."

The words "I'm close" are on the tip of my tongue, but are lost under the harsh screaming and moaning that tear out of me instead. My pussy grips his cock, my body shudders. Warmth radiates in waves from my slick center. Dante stills his frenzied movements as he releases, groaning out his pleasure.

"Karina."

His forehead touches mine and I unwrap my legs from

his waist. My body feels like jelly, but he steadies me so I don't melt onto the floor.

He steps away from me for a moment; when he returns, I realize my eyes were closed. I open to find Dante smiling at me.

"Wanted to fuck you so bad, I didn't even get you naked. That's a crime."

His fingers tease the hem of my sweater and I automatically lift my arms up. He hums in approval as he whisks my sweater off, and unhooks my bra. My hands move to the zipper of my skirt, but he stops me with a finger on my arm.

"Leave it on"

He slides a hand down the length of one of my braids, gently tugging out the band at the end and untwisting the strands. Then he does the same with the other braid.

His eyes never leave my body as he steps back. Both hands reach out and cup my breasts, thumbs rubbing over my nipples. "Yeah, you're just as perfect as I remembered."

In a few steps, we're next to his bed. He sits and reaches over to his desk, grabbing a blue velvet satchel. With a sly smile, he hands it to me. Curious and honestly a little nervous, I accept the bag. It's small, but has some heft. Untying the drawstrings, I peek inside. Confused, I stare at Dante.

"Never seen one before?"

"No." Gingerly, I grasp the cool metal and pull it out of the bag. It's sort of egg shaped, but heavier than any egg and it has a stem with a flared end. The flat part of the end is encrusted with pink jewels. It's sort of pretty.

Dante's intense gaze is still glued to my face. He holds

his hand out and I drop the thing into his palm. With his other hand, he pats his lap.

Yes, this is something I definitely missed. Draping myself over his lap settles my mind and makes my belly flutter at the same time. He spends a few minutes running his hand over the backs of my legs. Stroking and tickling. When I relax a little more he flips my skirt up, roughly palming my ass cheeks.

"Your ass is perfect."

"Thank you."

My thanks makes him chuckle. His body sways to the side and a drawer rolls open and closed.

*Crack!*

The palm of his hand connects with my ass and I moan. The warm sting prickles over my skin and I instinctively arch my back, offering myself to him. He spanks my other cheek then rubs the sting away with his hand.

"Were you a good girl while I was away?"

"Yes, daddy."

He slaps me again and again. The spanking intensifies but I love the sting and burn. I'm panting and moaning when he finally stops.

"Spread your legs," he says, his voice hoarse and rough.

I wiggle my thighs apart and his fingers gently stoke my wet folds.

"You really like that, don't you, baby girl." He's not asking me a question. Doesn't need to. The proof drips down his hand.

I moan louder as he presses a finger inside of me.

"You've got one greedy little cunt, baby girl. I just

fucked you against that door and you're already moaning for my cock again."

"Yes."

### Dante

Greedy cunt is an understatement. Karina's pussy is dripping after her spankin'. I've seen plenty of fucked up shit over the years. Never seen a girl who enjoyed gettin' spanked the way she does.

I'm real happy to be the one givin' it to her.

Tonight, I'm also gonna give her somethin' else.

Trailing my soaked fingers from her slick pussy up to her tight little asshole, I stop and use my other hand to pry her cheeks apart. She clenches and whines.

My hand delivers a sharp smack. "Relax."

She immediately relaxes.

I could get high off this girl's eagerness to please me.

Trembles of excitement work over her body. Rock hard nipples poke into my thigh. Holding her ass cheeks apart, I circle her hole with one finger, getting her used to my touch. When she relaxes a little more I press one finger inside. She whines and I retreat. Go back to softly stroking her.

"Gonna fuck this ass, Karina."

She whines, and I smack her butt. She's still sprawled out over my lap, but she tucks her arms under her chest and turns her face so her cheek is resting on the bed and looks up at me.

"It hurts."

She doesn't say, "Hell fucking no." Nope, my little bitch knows this is happening and wants me to take care of her.

"Not if I do it right." Picking up the anal plug, I run the smooth, tapered end over her lips. Her tongue darts out to lick it and I almost come in my pants.

"I'm gonna plug your ass to train it to take my cock."

Her eyes widen.

"This is the smallest one they make. I'll work you up to bigger ones until I think you're ready for me."

She moans and wriggles in my lap and my cock freaks the fuck out.

"It won't hurt?"

"No way would I hurt my baby girl. Gonna lube you up all nice and slick. When I finally claim that ass, you're gonna beg me to do it over and over."

She hesitates. "Okay." Her body relaxes and she even tips her ass up a little, as if she's offering herself.

I roll my eyes toward the ceiling. What the fuck did I do to deserve this little angel? She's like some gift I sure as fuck don't deserve.

It takes a second to wrap my head around how willing she is to please me. In an earlier part of my life, I might have taken advantage of the situation. But now? All I want to do is protect, and take care of Karina.

And fuck her every which way, of course.

"Have you done this before?" she asks softly.

"Not with anyone I cared about." Meaning, I'd never spent this much time and effort to get a bitch ready like I'm plannin' to do with her.

By the tight set of her lips, I can tell she's jealous and the evil prick inside me loves it.

This ain't all about her though. This is gonna be some long-drawn out, sick fuckin' foreplay for me as well. Thinking about her wearing a plug, getting ready to take my cock in her virgin asshole. It's going to be a test of willpower that I'm looking forward to. I get a head rush no alcohol or drug has ever given me.

Now that we're clear on the goal, I continue playing with her ass and loosening her up. When she relaxes, I click open the bottle of lube I set next to me and dribble it on her asshole, her skin puckers and dances as the cool liquid splashes down. Using two fingers, I massage all around her ass until she loosens up again, then I press one finger inside. A little more lube and I add a finger, stretching them apart and turning my hand.

Her lips part and she sighs a warm, happy noise. Christ, I'm harder than a motherfuckin' rock. My cock is beggin' me to quit this anal seduction bullshit and ram into her already.

"Like that, baby girl?"

"Mmmm."

"You're such a good girl, taking my fingers like this. So pretty over my lap."

"Thank you, daddy."

The plug is solid and cool in my hand. I press it to her lips. "Open. Warm it up with your mouth."

She licks it and then opens her mouth again and sucks. When she's done, I add more lube and begin working it into her ass. She squeals and wiggles, but I keep her steady with my arm around her waist. Finally, it pops into place. Little pink jewels wink at me from their spot nestled in her ass.

"You should see how pretty it looks."

She reaches back with one hand and touches it. "Are you sure I don't look silly?"

She's the hottest fucking thing in my universe, and she's asking me if she's looks silly.

"No, baby girl. It's taking all my self-control not to fuck you again."

"Why?"

Christ, she's killing me.

"Wanna go home with you."

She plants her feet on the floor and stands. "You don't have to stay here?" she asks.

"No."

Her mouth curves into a smile. Hooking my fingers into the waistband of her skirt, I pull her close and press a kiss to her stomach. "Take it off."

She unzips the skirt and lets it pool at her feet.

"You bring anything else to wear?"

"Yeah, I brought an outfit for tomorrow."

"Good. Go ahead and get dressed."

I don't think she's teasing me on purpose; but when she bends over bare-assed with that pink sparkly plug aimed at me, I have to count to ten.

"No panties," I tell her.

"Okay."

She slides into a skintight pair of leggings. Before I get the "what the fuck" out of my mouth, she slips on a sweatshirt long enough to cover her ass.

Okay then.

# CHAPTER THIRTEEN

**Karina**

The ride up to Dante's cabin is interesting. The plug—even though he said it's the smallest one—leaves me feeling very full and aware of my ass. Honestly, after the way he looked at me once he got the plug seated, I'm amazed we even made it out of the clubhouse. I thought for sure I was in for a night of being bent over and fucked every which way.

Who am I kidding? I'm sure that's still in the plans.

Sure enough, as soon as we enter the house, he's stripping off my clothes, leaning over to suck my nipples into his hot mouth. We end up on the couch, with me straddling his lap.

"Ride my cock, baby girl."

Planting my hands on his shoulders, I raise and lower myself until I scream out my release. Dante helps me up, and then bends me over the back of the couch, slamming his cock in me.

"This is so fuckin' hot," he grunts out as he twists and turns the plug in my ass. The dual sensations drive me crazy and I come again, bucking and calling out his name.

He groans and stops his frantic thrusting.

A sharp slap on my ass makes me giggle. He stalks out to the kitchen and returns to me with a smirk on his face. His strong arms lift me and he carries me upstairs while my fingers trace the lines of the bull tattooed on his chest.

"How long have you been in the MC?" I ask. He doesn't talk about the club with me very much, but I am curious about something that is such a big part of his life.

"Sixteen years. Started hanging around at sixteen. Got my prospect rocker at eighteen. Became a full-patched brother a year later."

He smiles down at me and sets me on the bed.

"Hands and knees, babe."

I roll over and do as he asks. He grabs the end of the plug and twists it. I can't believe how much he loves this thing. A twist in the opposite direction makes me moan. Then he tugs it out and retreats to the bathroom where I hear the water run for a while.

He chuckles and shakes his head when he comes out and finds me in the same position. "Up in bed, baby girl. Had a long fuckin' day and I am ready to go to sleep holdin' my girl."

He's so sweet. I can't get under the covers fast enough. He pulls me close and nestles me against his side. The lamp clicks off, and I feel his hand stroking over my hair and back. "Can't believe I've gotten so used to this already. Fuckin' hated bein' away from you."

It's the second time he said something like that tonight. Inside I'm glowing with pride that he feels this way about me.

"Me too," I whisper. "I missed you."

"Were you nervous being alone up here?"

I think about it. I was a little scared the first night. "Not too bad. I made sure I was inside before dark and that helped."

He hugs me a little tighter. "Good, 'cause I gotta go on another run next week. Gonna be short like this one, but still."

"That's okay," I tell him. "I'll be fine."

"I know."

We fall asleep holding each other.

### Dante

CHURCH IS QUICK THIS WEEK. Hemi won't even look my way. Good. The fucker finally learned his lesson. His split lip and black eye give me a measure of comfort.

We divide up the runs that need to happen this week. I've got seniority so I pull the shortest one out to Cherry Valley. It's not an easy territory, but it's not as rough as what Hemi's facing again. I smirk when he opens his mouth to whine about it.

"We've all done our time making that delivery and pick-up," Romeo snaps.

Luck will go with me to Cherry Valley. Wolf volunteers to ride with Hemi.

We break, and Prez calls me back.

"How's the hot lil' bitch doing? Ready to pass her off yet?"

"Fuck no." I respect my Prez, but his comments about my girl are startin' to piss me off. I jerk my head toward one of our older members. "You talk about Mug's ol' lady like that?"

He rears back, clearly surprised. Fuck, so am I.

"If she looked like Karina, yeah, I probably would."

I fuckin' hate the way her name sounds comin' out of his mouth. Fuck, I hate he remembered her name. Can't remember the last time he even used a woman's actual name. They were all babes, honeys, and bitches to him.

"Besides, you said she ain't your ol' lady yet."

"Well she's in my house, in my bed, and on my bike." I point at the table. "Only thing missin' is a club claiming and she ain't ready for that yet."

"All right. Calm the fuck down. Won't say another word about her hot little ass, okay?"

I growl and flip him off, which only makes him laugh. Stalking into main room, I spot Hemi gettin' sucked off on the couch. Okay. Could have done without that. On closer inspection, I see it's Sadie doin' the suckin' and I fucking laugh. Bitch wasted no time replacing me. And if Hemi thinks this is some sort of turnabout, he's mistaken.

I grab my cell phone out of the box our VP makes us drop them into before every meeting and head home.

Karina pulls into the driveway behind me. She squeals and runs over as soon as she gets out of her car. "Dante," she yells flinging herself against me so hard, she almost knocks us over.

Can't help laughing at how excited she is to see me. Told her I'd be back real late tonight. Now I'm glad my plans changed.

She pulls back and peppers the side of my face with kisses. Fisting my hand in her hair, I hold her still and take her mouth.

Pink stains her cheeks and she's panting when I finally let her go.

"I'm so happy you're home early."

"Me too, baby girl."

I tip my head up, the clear blue sky calls to me. "Let's go for a ride."

Her mouth curves in an excited grin and she claps her hands. "Can I go change first?"

"Yeah, of course. Make sure you grab a sweatshirt."

She nods and runs inside.

Less than ten minutes later, she's flyin' out the front door. I hand over her helmet and help her strap it on.

Having her at my back feels right. The weather's perfect. We've got a few more hours of daylight and I know exactly where I want to take her.

# CHAPTER FOURTEEN

**Karina**

THE COOL AIR RUSHING OVER ME IS REFRESHING after being cooped up in school all day, but I'm glad Dante told me to grab a sweatshirt. He takes us out of the city and eventually we wind our way into one of the state parks. The barrier with the "closed" sign is no obstacle for him or the bike. He swerves around it and keeps on driving.

After a few miles through trees, the road veers to the left and opens into a wide parking lot. A large lake is visible on our right. He glides the bike to a stop and sets his feet down. I hop off and wait for him to join me.

"How come the park is empty?"

"State can't afford to keep it open year-round."

"Oh."

He takes my hand and leads me to the water's edge.

"I'd say let's skinny dip, but it's a little cold."

I try not to drool over the idea of seeing Dante naked in

the great outdoors. "I wouldn't mind skinny-dipping with you."

He advances until we're standing so close you couldn't insert a sheet of paper between us.

"That right, baby girl?"

"Yup."

"Show me."

My mouth twitches, but I can't hold back my smile. I'm nervous someone might catch us, but I also trust Dante to keep me safe and protect me. Very slowly, I peel my clothes off, relishing the way his eyes narrow as he watches me. Once I start working my jeans down my legs, he springs into action and undresses. Taking my hand, he leads me into the water. Instantly my teeth chatter as the cold water laps at my ankles, then my legs, and up to my waist. Dante's eyes go straight to my breasts as my nipples harden.

"Very nice," he growls, dragging me farther out into the water. When I can barely touch, he stops and pulls me close.

"Better?" he asks, trailing his fingers over my breasts. His fingers pinch and roll my nipples until I'm moaning in his arms. Hooking an arm around my waist, he pulls me tight, leaning down to suck on one nipple, then the other.

All that cool water sliding over my naked skin makes me brazen. Even though I'm cold, my skin tingles with heat. My legs wrap around his waist, my hips grinding and searching. Finally, my core bumps up against his cock.

"You want that, baby girl?"

"Yes, please."

He squeezes his eyes shut. "Fuck," he mutters,

reaching down to guide himself to my entrance. His lips descend on mine, his tongue taking ownership of my mouth. Hot and throbbing, his cock stretches me so good as he slides in.

Ripping his mouth from mine, he stares into my eyes. "Love fuckin' you bare, baby."

So that's why everything feels so intense. "Yes," I answer, frantically trying to gain some leverage.

"Still takin' your pills like a good girl?"

"Yes, daddy."

He grunts in approval, his hands gripping my waist, holding me tight for his thrusts. I wrap my legs around him tighter and just let myself go. Dante takes a few steps closer to shore. Up and down, he guides me over his cock. I'm so close, but can't get enough friction and whine in frustration. Dante's eyes open, searching my face. He slows his movements and guides one hand to my clit, pressing and rubbing, while I grind my hips into him.

He leans down; light beard stubble grazes my cheek. His tongue flicks my earlobe. "That's it. Come all over my bare dick. Your hot fuckin' pussy is choking my dick, baby girl. Feels so good," he growls against my neck.

His filthy words finally trigger my orgasm and I moan long and loud. Dante's hands return to my hips and a few short strokes later, he comes with a roar. My forehead drops to his shoulder, while my arms hug him tight.

Still joined together, he carries me out of the water. He sets me down on a picnic table and I sigh when we lose our connection. "Stay right there," he orders.

He returns with his jeans on, but unbuttoned. Droplets of water cling to his colorfully inked skin. Our clothes fisted in one hand. He takes his T-shirt and pats me dry before dressing me. When we're both fully dressed, Dante kisses my forehead. His hand cups my cheek, thumb rubbing over my skin. I close my eyes and lean into his touch.

"How was school today?" he asks.

"Okay," I murmur.

"Anything exciting happen?"

"Not really."

"That sounds like a 'yes, but I don't want to tell you' to me," he says, a dark chuckle following his words.

Finally, opening my eyes, I glance up at him. "Athena's mad at me because I don't want to go to prom."

He cocks his head, dark eyes narrowing "Why don't you want to go?"

I'm shocked he's asking. Isn't the answer obvious? How could I go to prom with someone else? And I know there's no way in hell he's going to prom with me.

"I, uh—"

"You need a dress?"

"Well, yes, but—"

"What?"

"I didn't think you'd want to go." There I said it.

The laughter I expected doesn't come. His face remains stone-cold serious. "I don't. But that doesn't mean *you* can't go. Don't some of you all just get together and go in groups?"

"Yeah, I guess." I tilt my head up. "You won't be mad if I go?"

His eyebrows draw down in a deep frown. "No. Why the fuck would I be mad?"

"I don't know."

He settles his big hands over my shoulders and crouches down so we're eye to eye. "Babe, you plannin' to fuck someone else at your prom?"

"No! Of course not."

"Then why would I have a problem with it?"

"Okay, okay."

He shakes his head at me. "Here, seems like a good time to give you this." He reaches into his pocket, pulling out a credit card and handing it to me. My name is embossed on the front.

"What's this?"

"Wanna make sure you're taken care of when I'm outta town. Don't want you feeling like you gotta ask me for money when you need something—like a friggin' prom dress." He pins me with a hard stare. "I think I can trust you not to abuse it."

He doesn't phrase it as a question, but I answer anyway. "Of course not."

"Use it for whatever you need. Gas, food, goin' to lunch with your friend, school stuff." He runs a hand over my hair, picking up the strands and letting them slip through his fingers. "Buy whatever girly shit you need. It's tied to a checking account. I'll get an alert when the account gets below a certain amount, and stuff more cash in it. Okay?"

This is huge. I'm completely overwhelmed. "Thank you." My gaze drops to the ground.

"Hey." His knuckles brush my chin, tilting my head up. "Look at me."

Unable to resist the pull of his voice, I peek up at him through my lashes.

"Told you I'd look after you and I meant it."

## Dante

Hadn't planned to get carried away and fuck Karina in a freezing cold lake. Seems I can be ready to stick my dick in her at any time, any place.

The memory of being skin on skin with her has me hard again.

The sun's setting as we leave the park. We ride farther away from home. Part of me just wants to keep going. Start this week's run early. Take my little bitch with me.

But no, she ain't ready for that. And she's got school tomorrow.

School. Fuckin' hell. High school fucking prom. Can't believe she—what? Thought I wouldn't let her go? Fuck that. I'm half entertaining the idea of actually taking her. Wouldn't that shock the hell out of my baby girl?

We stop at a small sandwich shop for dinner. Both of us have soup to warm up. Watching Karina purse her sexy lips and blow on her spoon has me thinking all sorts of nasty thoughts.

"Got homework, baby girl?"

"A little bit."

Guess I'll have to wait for my blowjob.

"You know I'm leavin' tomorrow mornin' right?"

Her lips quirk into a brief pout, but she smooths it out quickly and nods. She's gonna miss me, but she's tryin' to act all brave and shit. Cute.

"Yeah," she answers.

"I'll be back Friday night. Probably late."

Now her mouth turns down. "Oh."

We get back early enough for her to finish her schoolwork. I give her a good face fucking before tucking her into bed. After the lights are off, she inches closer to me until I wrap her up in my arms.

"You need to come, baby girl?"

She whines something that sounds like a yes.

Slipping my hand into her underwear, I find her clit and work her gently. After a couple minutes, she's moaning, spreading her legs, and bumping her hips up.

I'm hard as a motherfuckin' rock already, so I pull her up on top of me. She wastes no time working my dick into her snug cunt. Riding me like she's got a gun to her head.

"Oh, fuck, Dante! Fuck," she yelps. The grin on my face is huge. Not that she can tell in the dark.

When her tight muscles spasm around me, I shoot my fuckin' load deep inside her. Her soft little sigh as she drapes her body over mine, tightens my chest. She nuzzles against me, and presses kisses along my neck and cheek.

"Thank you, daddy," she whispers.

Patting her ass, I pull her off my softening cock and she rolls to the side.

"Will you be a good girl while I'm away?"

"Yes, I promise."

I roll over to kiss her cheek and gather her close. Never fuckin' liked sleepin' with a woman before.

Now, I can't sleep unless I got my girl in my arms.

# CHAPTER FIFTEEN

**Karina**

I'M SO EXCITED TO GET HOME THIS AFTERNOON. Dante texted this morning and said he should be home for dinner. He has to stop at the clubhouse first and then he's coming home to spend the weekend with me.

Before leaving for school, I pulled out a crock-pot and threw in a package of chicken breasts. As soon as I get home, I add in a jar of green salsa, jalapenos, an onion, and some other ingredients. I realize I'm missing a few things, so I grab my purse and run down to the local market.

When I get back, a motorcycle I don't recognize is in the driveway. At first, I'm scared. Then I see Logan sitting on the porch. As much as we don't seem to get along lately, he'd never hurt me.

"What are you doing here?" I call out. Walking around to the back of my car, I pull out my grocery bags.

Logan stomps down off the porch. "So it's true? You really are living with him?"

"Yes." I barely hold in my gasp when I take in his face. The fight he got into with Dante last week was pretty bad, but he should have healed by now.

"What happened?"

"Got into some trouble on the run I just got back from."

I don't know what to say to that.

He jerks his chin. "He buy you a fuckin' car?"

I'm not liking his tone, but I answer anyway. "Yeah, so I can get to school."

"Christ, Karina, I never pictured you turnin' into a fuckin' whore."

Pain slashes through me. He's taking the nice things Dante's done for me and turning them into something ugly. Even though he can be pretty kinky, Dante's never once made me feel dirty or ashamed about *anything*. With one sentence, Logan makes me doubt everything.

I'm furious, but I don't know how to respond.

"Don't be such an asshole," I finally snap back.

He shakes his head as he approaches me. "Dante sent me. Club's on lockdown. Go inside and grab some stuff. I gotta bring you to our safe house."

What? What the hell does that mean? And I don't believe for a second Dante would trust Logan to take me anywhere.

"Why didn't he call and tell me himself?"

Logan rolls his eyes like I'm the stupidest girl he's ever met. "He ain't got time to deal with you. This is big shit he's gotta handle. Be thankful he even remembered to send me at all."

Tears sting my eyes. While that's probably true, it hurts to hear it. Especially from Logan.

He rests his hands on my shoulders and stares into my eyes. Maybe he senses his harsh words hurt my feelings, because his tone is much gentler. "Come on. Go grab enough stuff to get you through to Monday. Dante's going to meet us up there."

"Maybe I should call him and see if he wants me to bring anything for him?"

"Can't. He's in a meeting with Romeo. Won't answer his phone. Go on, hurry up."

Something's wrong. But I'm not sure what to do. As soon as I get upstairs, I lock myself in the bathroom and try to call Dante. It goes straight to voicemail. In the past, Dante has explained all the guys hand over their cell phones before sitting down for "church".

Maybe Logan is telling the truth.

I speak as softly as possible, in case Logan followed me inside. "Dante, it's me. Logan's here. He says you sent him to take me to a safe house because the club is on lockdown? Are you sure you want me to go with him? I don't know—"

"Karina! Let's go!" Logan shouts from downstairs.

"If you get this in the next few minutes, text me and let me know it's okay to go with him," I say in a rush and hit end.

I stare at my phone for a few seconds. Something doesn't feel right. There are probably twenty other people Dante would choose to come get me before going to Logan. But what if he did send him because something so bad is going down? Maybe he had no choice?

Without realizing it, my hand's squeezing my phone so tight, my fingers press the volume button down and the phone buzzes in my hand, startling me. I stare at it again, willing it to ring.

Banging on the bathroom door rattles me so hard I drop the phone. "Karina, stop fucking around, we gotta go. What are you doing?"

"I'm going to the bathroom. Jeez, give me a minute!" I shout back.

Jamming my phone into my pocket, I hustle over and flush the toilet. While running the water, I grab a few things I think I'll need. My birth control pills for sure. Vitamins, face wash, toothbrush, toothpaste, shampoo, conditioner, soap. I glance at Dante's side of the vanity. He'd probably like some of his stuff too, right? I grab shaving cream, a razor, his toothbrush...and that's all I can think of. I shove everything into a couple cosmetic bags and exit the bathroom.

Logan's standing in the middle of the room staring at the bed.

"What are you doing in here?" I ask.

"I can't believe you really fucking sleep with him, Karina."

Brushing past him, I dump my armload on the bed. "That's none of your business."

"Come on, hurry up."

"I'm hurrying." Snatching my backpack off the floor, I stuff some clothes in. Logan finally wanders out and I scurry over to Dante's nightstand. Yanking open the drawer, I grab the small bottle of lube and the jeweled anal plug. No reason we can't have fun while we're hiding out

—or whatever this is about. I can't wait to see the look on his face when he sees what I brought.

I pull out my phone and check it one last time. Nothing from Dante. This time I shoot him a quick text.

*Leaving house w/Logan now. See u soon.*

For some reason, I mute the phone before sticking it back in my pocket.

Logan's waiting on the front porch, and takes my backpack when I step outside. He holds out his hand. "Give me your phone, and I'll let Dante know we're leaving."

No way am I handing over my phone to him.

"Oh, shoot, I forgot it." I turn to go back inside, but he stops me.

"Don't worry about it. I got mine. Just need to charge it."

"Okay."

His gaze darts back and forth between his bike and my car. "We'll take your car."

"Okay."

He seems indecisive. "I'll drive."

"Fine." I tug the keys out of my pocket and hand them over.

## Dante

ALL HELL BROKE LOOSE on Hemi's Mexican run. The fucker got out of jail and made it over the border. But he's been MIA since.

Romeo's fuckin' livid.

We're all sittin' around the table trying to figure out what to do. Little fucker was supposed to be bringin' a package back with him and no one knows if it was confiscated when he got picked up.

"All right, let's set that aside," Romeo orders, taking control of the meeting once again. He points at me. "How'd it go?"

"In and out."

"Any witnesses?"

"Fuck no." I pull out the envelope of cash I collected after the job and toss it on the table.

Romeo hands it off to our treasurer, Savage. I know I'll get my cut before I leave this room, so I ain't too worried.

I flick my wrist over to see the time—something that doesn't go unnoticed by Romeo. Karina should be home from school by now. Missed my girl and want to get home to see her. Hemi goin' missing is fuckin' up my afternoon plans.

Romeo dismisses everyone except our VP—Wolf, road captain—Whip, Savage, Viper, Luck, and me.

Romeo points at Savage and jerks his head at me. Savage hands over my envelope of cash, which I stuff into an inside pocket of my cut.

"What're we gonna do 'bout Hemi?" Luck asks.

Romeo shakes his head, and then nods at Wolf.

"Boy was shook up, but we made it across the border fine. He fuckin' split when we stopped for a refuel."

"Could he have been grabbed?" Whip asks.

Wolf shrugs. "I guess. But his bike was gone, too. I wasn't in the store but a minute."

Savage glances my way. "He think we're gonna be mad he got picked up?"

"How the fuck should I know?" I growl. "Ain't no reason to take off like a pussy. We've all done our time. Kinda a given in our line of work."

Romeo smirks at that. "I got feelers out to our supports and other charters from here to the border."

Viper finally decides to add his two cents. "Maybe he met up with a hot piece of ass and wanted to get laid instead of comin' and gettin' bitched out here. He spent lots of time bitching about the lack of pussy on our last run."

"That better be it," Romeo says.

Because nothing else makes sense. Unless he decided to turn on us.

Romeo releases us with an order to stay close.

"Yeah, I'll be at my cabin," I answer.

His mouth twists into a filthy grin. "Yeah, figure you'll be balls deep in jailbait pussy."

"Fuck you."

Luck claps me on the back as we walk out and collect our cell phones from the basket outside the door.

"How's your girl? She okay with you bein' away?" Luck asks.

I know he ain't askin' to be a dick. "Think so. Her dad wasn't home much, so I think she's used to it. Still want to get home and see her though."

The corners of his mouth curl up in a genuine smile. "Yeah, don't blame you."

He says something else, but I'm distracted by my phone goin' off as soon as I turn it back on. Got a voicemail and text from Karina.

The text comes up first. Sent almost an hour ago.

**Karina: Leaving house w/Logan now. See u soon.**

What the actual fuck?

My vision clouds red.

Murder must be written on my face. "What's wrong, brother?" Luck asks.

I put my finger up and dial into my voicemail. Hitting speaker so we can both listen, I hold the phone out. Romeo walks out as soon as the message starts playing.

Karina's hushed voice is hard to make out at first, but I get the gist of what's going on.

*"Dante, it's me. Logan's here. He says you sent him to take me to a safe house because the club is on lockdown. Are you sure you want me to go with him? I don't know—"*

She stops for some reason. A muffled shout sounds from somewhere in the background. Motherfuckin' Hemi, no doubt.

*"If you get this in the next few minutes, text me and let me know it's okay to go with him."*

"Motherfucker!" I jab my finger at Romeo. "He's dead. That motherfucker is dead. He laid a fuckin' hand on my woman. It's grounds and you fuckin' know it."

Romeo holds up his hands. "I hear you. Let's get the whole story—"

"What fuckin' whole story? He fuckin' tricked her—"

Luck puts his hand on my arm to stop me. Much calmer than I am, he says, "Prez, you heard the girl. Hemi told her a fuckin' lie to get her to go with him. That can't stand."

"He fuckin' touches her, he's not just *out bad*. He's fuckin' *dead*." I ain't makin' idle threats either. Whatever Hemi's doin' goes beyond disrespectin' a brother. He's outright pissing on our code.

I'm shaking with rage. Proud of my fuckin' girl though. She did good. Knew something was wrong and called me first. I need to get to her. Need to touch her. Make sure she's okay. Hemi's obviously lost his fuckin' mind. I'm scared shitless he'll do something to hurt her.

Fear ain't something I've felt in a long time. I mete out justice with my fists for the club. Fucking *kill* for my club. So no, there ain't much I fear in this world.

Losing Karina? Fucking terrifies me.

A small voice inside me says *this is why*. This is why I shouldn't ever have gotten involved with a bitch.

# CHAPTER SIXTEEN

### Karina

WE'RE NOT IN THE CAR VERY LONG BEFORE I conclude I'm in trouble. Logan won't give me any details about where we're going. He won't talk to me at all.

We head southeast out of the city and I pay close attention so I'll be able to tell Dante.

After driving for an hour and a half, I start squirming in my seat.

"Logan, I need to go to the bathroom."

"Can't you wait?"

"Uh, no."

"We've got maybe another hour."

I twist and make a show out of crossing my legs. "Definitely not."

He blows out a breath. "Fine. There's a rest stop coming up."

He pulls up to the curb. "Hurry back," he instructs as I jump out of the car.

It must be a busy traveling day or something because the bathroom is jammed and I have to wait. When a stall finally opens, I lock myself in it and whip out my phone. I've got at least ten missed calls from Dante and one text.

*Dante: Don't go with Hemi.*

*Shit! I knew it.*

As I tap out Dante's number, my fingers are shaking so much I almost drop the phone in the toilet.

"Karina!" he shouts. "Where are you, baby girl? Are you okay?"

"We're at the San Silas rest stop."

Someone bangs on the stall door. "Hurry up. There's people waitin'."

"Fuck. Dante, hold on." Holding my phone at my side, I step out. A mom with two kids gives me a bitchy look, but I ignore her and walk into the food court. Even above the noise of the rest stop, I hear Dante's voice yelling from my phone. Huddling facing the wall, out of the way of traffic, I put the phone up to my ear.

"Sorry, Dante. I needed to—"

"Karina. Stay where you are. Luck and I are on our way."

"Okay—"

Something hard presses into my back. Warm breath skates over my ear and down my neck. "Thought you forgot your phone, sprite?" Logan whispers. "Don't fuckin' move."

"Karina? What's wrong, baby girl?"

Logan slips my phone out of my hand and ends the call

without a word. My phone disappears into his pocket. "Move," he growls in my ear. "Signal anyone and I'll shoot you."

"Logan," I plead. "Why are you doing this?"

"Start walking, Karina. I'm not fucking around."

He slips an arm around my waist, and I guess to any casual observer we must look like a young couple in love. Although, if anyone bothered to look closely at my face, it would be obvious that's not true.

When we get to the car, he presses me up against the driver's side door. "You're driving. Don't pull any stunts."

I'm too scared to come up with any sort of plan that doesn't involve crashing—which I'd rather avoid—or getting shot.

So I drive.

I steer us back onto Interstate 10. "Where are we going?"

"Just keep driving."

After a couple miles, he breaks the silence. "What did you say to Dante?"

"I told him where we were."

His fist slams into the door. "Fuck! This is bad. He'll fuckin' kill me."

"Well then maybe you shouldn't have kidnapped me."

He's silent, so I risk glancing over. His eyes are fixed on me and it freaks me out.

"Why did you have to come there?"

"Where?"

"The clubhouse. That first day. Why?"

I shrug. I don't want to admit that I originally went there to make him jealous.

"What can you possibly see in him?"

He can't be serious. "Dante?"

"Who else?"

"He's good to me. He takes care of me."

"Are you fuckin' kidding? He's an animal. You know he was so pissed with me, he sent me down to Mexico to get killed?"

I open my mouth to call bullshit, except I wonder if it's true. Then I decide I don't care. My shoulders lift in a nervous shrug.

"You really want me dead, sprite?"

"Stop calling me that. I don't care enough about you to want you dead."

He lets out a heavy sigh. "Karina—"

"Don't. You made it clear how you felt about me."

"You don't understand."

Now it's my turn to sigh. "I don't want to hear it."

He bolts forward in his seat. "There. Get off this exit."

I steer us onto the off-ramp and he directs me to a shabby looking motel.

"Really?" I'm striving for a bored tone, but I think I sound scared.

"I gotta stop and think. The club's gonna be after me by now. Pull up to the front door."

As the car rolls to a stop, he pulls up the emergency brake and takes the keys. "Wait here and don't move. We need to talk."

Don't move. Where the fuck am I supposed to go? We're in the middle of nowhere and he took my damn phone.

He's in and out pretty quick. "Drive 'round back," he says as he gets back in the car.

My heart stops when he opens the door to our room. There's one bed.

All I can think about is that one bed. "You can't be serious."

He shakes his head and pushes me inside, locking the door behind him. He sets his black duffel bag down on the cheap, scarred-up dresser. "Sit," he orders. I take out a chair at the table and drop into it. My legs won't stop shaking. I want to show him how indifferent I am, so I stare at the grungy, green curtains.

That's a mistake.

Logan takes my arms and pulls them behind my back. As soon as his hands circle my biceps, I squeal and try to get away, but he's too strong. "Stay still."

He works quickly, tying me to the damn chair. It's not uncomfortable yet, but it will be.

When he's finished, he takes the chair across from me.

"Now you're going to hear my side of things."

Dante and Karina's story continues in
Disconnect (Iron Bulls MC #2)

# ALSO BY PHOENYX SLAUGHTER

Asunder (Iron Bulls MC #1)

Disconnect (Iron Bulls MC #2)

Entwined (Iron Bulls MC #3)

Vexed (Iron Bulls MC #4)

Unhinged (Iron Bulls MC #5)

Dirty Side Down (Iron Bulls MC Boxed Set #1)

Infatuation

# ACKNOWLEDGMENTS

Thank you to Hot Tree Editing for a fabulous editing experience.

My Beta Readers: Alison, Amber, Kelli, Kim and Melony. Thank you for taking time out of your busy lives to read Asunder and give me feedback. I wasn't completely confident I would publish this until you ladies got a hold of it!

I hope you enjoyed Asunder. I set out to create something fun and filthy with an alpha hero who was crude, yet loving (in his own way).

Thank you for purchasing and reading my novella. If you loved Asunder, a review would mean the world to me!

Thank you!